Laughing Gravy

Sarvananda

(Alastair Jessiman)

*Best wishes –
Sarvānanda*

To Satyadaka

Laughing Gravy
Forty years of comic writing

Sarvananda
(Alastair Jessiman)

Laughing Gravy

Copyright © 1982 – 2024.Sarvananda (Alastair Jessiman)

All rights reserved.

ISBN 9798336344554

All rights reserved. No part of this publication may be reproduced or utilised in any form or by any means, electronic or mechanical, including photocopying, microfilm, recording, or by any information storage and retrieval system, or used in another book, without written permission from the author.

The plays in this anthology may be performed with the permission of the author.

Published by *Triratna InHouse Publications*
www.*triratna-inhouse-publications.org*

TRIRATNA
INHOUSE
PUBLICATIONS

Contents

Introduction and thanks 7

Stories
Ian makes a friend 10
Ask the Doc 13
Stand up tragedy 16
Smart cookie 18
Macnab is a bitter man 19
My name is Anguish 22
Rejection 25
White Rabbit 27
Angel Pie 29
Just in case 31
Lemons and Lemmings 33
Improve your breakfast 36
The Tourist's Guide to Hell 38
Anorak 42
Creosote 43
Infestation 45
The raising of Lazarus 48
Prime numbers 52

Plays and monologues
A short lecture on comedy 60
Angulimala: Portrait of a Serial Killer 64
A short sermon 78

Family Values 81
Superhero 89
Death: a case for the defence 93
Concluding remarks 105

Articles 109
Defying the spirit of gravity 110
First loves: Just William 117

Fictional autobiography
From Lawrence of Suburbia 122

Poems and lyrics
A cautionary tale of Tom, who denied his own nature
and became a vegetable 136
Selkie 141
Fine thanks 143
Strange things happen to me 146
Toad 149

Final words
Famous last words 154
Apocalypse the noo 158
Indestructible Bob 161

Introduction and thanks

Laughing Gravy consists of stories, short plays, monologues, lyrics, essays, and semi-autobiographical pieces, all of which I've written over the last forty years or so. What they have in common is, firstly, that they're all intended to be comic and secondly, that they never earned me any money. I hope you enjoy this selection, secure in the knowledge that, by purchasing my book, you're both supporting the arts and assisting me financially (to half of the price of a haircut.)

I've been very lucky to have been involved in three very good writing groups over the years: *Octagon Writers*, *The Angels* and *Rainbow Writers*. My writing colleagues have given me very valuable feedback, and generally been very supportive and kind. I'd particularly like to thank my writing buddy, Bruce Peterkin, as well as Satyadaka, co-conspirator, frequent collaborator and invaluable adviser. Also a big thank you to Lokabandhu for all his help in preparing this book for publication.

The first person to contact me and adequately explain the title of this anthology, (with particular reference to the comedians involved and the animal they have befriended), will receive a tube of *Smarties*. Vegan alternative on request. Strictly no Googling.

Stories

"Everything lasts too long except life," some wit remarked. I tend to agree, and I prefer to write – and read – short stories which are very short indeed. It gives you time to do other things like phone a friend or unblock the sink. So, you will find these stories, (the first drafts of which were usually written very quickly and in a state of manic exuberance), mercifully brief. I've also included a longer story, *Prime Numbers,* which is a favourite of mine.

Ian makes a friend

Despite having seven hundred and thirty Facebook friends, Ian was lonely. He decided that what he needed was a *real* friend, not just somebody to exchange messages with online. So, he bought a catapult, got a half brick from a skip, and read up on first aid. That Saturday evening, as a cyclist was passing his house, Ian shot a half brick from his catapult. The brick, as planned, hit the front wheel of the bike and the cyclist was pitched on to the road. Ian immediately rushed out with his first aid bag and administered to the man who was bleeding from the knees. After putting plasters on the man's knees, Ian invited his new friend for a cup of soothing tea. The man's name turned out to be Maurice Parkinson and he was grateful to Ian and so agreed when Ian suggested they meet up for coffee some time.

Ian was very excited that his plan had worked so the next day he did the same thing, that is, shot a half brick at a passing cyclist. This time the brick struck the cyclist on the head. Ian rushed out, as before, and guided the semi-conscious woman in question to his flat where he gave her soothing tea before contacting the emergency services. The lady said she thought her name was Deirdre, but couldn't swear on it. They exchanged mobile numbers.

Soon Ian had lots of friends, (although admittedly a few of them were so badly injured that they were unable to communicate effectively.) Eventually, Ian thought it would be a good idea to have a party for all his new friends, so he bought some huge packets of nuts and crisps and some bottles of vodka and phoned everybody up and yes, he had a party. Maurice Parkinson was there and Deirdre, (although her name turned out to be Janet), and Sergeant Muffin, who was in the army, and wee Davie MacAllister, who was studying to become a zoologist, and a Russian bloke, and the famous actor, Kieffer Sutherland, and the lady from the Post

Office and the Garibaldi twins, who had a tandem, and Sir Allardyce Glenfinning M.P., and many, many more.

Unfortunately, the party turned out to be a huge mistake because people occasionally asked one another *"How do you come to know Ian?"* and, of course, the reply was invariably, *"He helped me out after some hooligan knocked me off my bike with a brick."* So, very soon, Ian's ruse was discovered and he was confronted by all and sundry. Ian apologised and told the assembled company how lonely he had been but this didn't appease the collective wrath and he was eventually taken to court and convicted of conspiracy to defraud the public, grievous bodily harm and buckling seventy-three bicycle wheels.

Ian was sent to prison for three months. He suspected he wouldn't make many friends in prison and, indeed, he found his sentence very difficult at first because people teased him. His cellmate, David Grubb, who was in prison for stealing five hundred boxes of digestive biscuits, was the worst. He teased Ian about his teeth, the size of his head and his inability to pronounce the letter "R." Also, there was a man in prison called "Bastard" Harris, who seemed to rule the roost. He was a notorious gang leader and everybody was afraid of him, even the guards. Rumour had it that he had killed twenty-five people, (although rumour also had it that he had his tender side.) Ian started to notice that Bastard Harris was always watching him. Wherever Ian went, there was Bastard Harris with his flat nose and his tattoos and his scars. In the food hall Bastard Harris would always sit opposite Ian and just stare at him. Ian became very frightened.

One day Ian came back from the kitchen, where he'd been scrubbing pans, to find a small chocolate and a red rose on his pillow. David Grubb and his belongings had disappeared. Someone else's jacket was lying on David Grubb's bunk.

Then Bastard Harris came into the cell with a cardboard box which had things in it like his toothbrush, his cigarettes, his lucky plastic giraffe, his knuckle duster and his playing cards.

"I'm your new cellmate," said Bastard Harris.

Ian looked at the chocolate and the rose on his pillow. Then he looked at Bastard Harris who blushed a deep crimson and stared at his feet.

Ask the Doc

Dr. Hamilton Crust M.D., the Online Doc, answers your queries.

Dear Dr. Crust,

Recently my wife has taken to lying in in the mornings. In fact, for the last four days, I have been unable to wake her at all. Her other symptoms include a very cold and pale skin, extreme stiffness which lasted forty-eight hours before wearing off, the discharge of an unusual liquid from some of her orifices, swelling in the stomach and, particularly in the last twenty-four hours, the emanation of an unusual and unsavoury aroma. Should I be concerned?

Ted Willis – Swindon.

Dear Ted Willis,

I'm afraid that is sounds as if your spouse has, (as we in the medical profession say), "passed on." This happens to everyone and should not be particularly alarming. I would advise that you call the local undertaker however, before things get *significantly* out of hand. As for how concerned you should be, that depends on how much you valued your wife

The Doc.

Dear Doc,

Recently I had an almost total cardio vascular collapse after eating a packet of *Spangles*. I had discovered these boiled sweets in a drawer of my father's desk after his death, and they immediately recalled my childhood. So, I ate them. During my long recovery, investigations on the Internet revealed that *Spangles* were discontinued in 1984. Is it possible that some foodstuffs can make you ill if consumed decades after purchasing? I also found an *Aztec* bar and a *Fry's Five Centre* in my father's desk. I remember these chocolate bars fondly. They are calling to me.

Sincerely,

Gumbo

Dear Gumbo,

It's inadvisable to consume sweetmeats forty years after they were purchased. I would put the *Aztec* bar and the *Fry's Five Centre* in the compost bin immediately if I were you. Do you think your father may have harboured *many* out-of-date consumables? Is this possibly the reason for his passing? Nostalgia can often be a genetic condition and can be very dangerous, especially as regards foodstuffs. Be warned. I knew three generations of a family - grandmother, son and grandson - who were all struck down after sharing a 1973 Wombles *Toffo* Easter Egg washed down with bottles of cherry flavoured *Panda Pops* (discontinued 2011.)

The Doc

Dear Dr. Crust,

Recently I have become worried about the size of my husband's head. It didn't worry me before but, about a week ago, it just suddenly came to me that his head seemed huge. (Perhaps I have been in denial for years.) My husband and I don't go out much as we are both quite elderly and I wobble so I can't compare his head to anybody else's head at the moment. However, we do watch a lot of old black and white movies and, to go by the heads of the stars of yesteryear, e.g. Clark Gable, Humphrey Bogarde, Kenneth More etc., my husband's head does seem to be very big indeed. Of course, to be a Hollywood star in those days might have demanded that you have a *particularly* well shaped head so perhaps comparisons are odious in this respect. Still, I remain troubled. I am enclosing a picture of my husband and myself taken in Paris in happier days when I was not worried about the size of his head. What do you think? Is his head abnormally large? If it is, is it dangerous? Am I making a mountain out of a molehill?

Betty Drangle, Edinburgh

PS I have just measured my husband's head. It is 75 centimetres in circumference.

Dear Mrs. Drangle,

In the picture, your husband's head does not seem abnormally large. You also do not say if he himself is worried. To go by the photograph, he does not look the worried type. In fact, he looks very cheery. Whereas, if I may say so, you yourself look rather anxious. Why not take a leaf from your husband's book? Heads come in all shapes and sizes. I have just measured my own head and it is quite a few centimetres larger than your husband's head so unless my head is abnormally large, I don't think you have anything to worry about.

The Doc

Dear Mrs. Drangle,

Subsequent to my previous reply, I have just found out, after talking to a colleague, that my head *is* abnormally large and I have been referred to a head specialist.

The Doc

Stand up tragedy

What did Sid James, Tommy Cooper and the French playwright and actor, Moliere, have in common?

I'll tell you. They all died on stage. Sid James had a heart attack while performing a farce in Sunderland. Tommy Cooper collapsed in the middle of a live, televised performance at *Her Majesty's Theatre* and got a huge laugh. The laughs kept coming until they realised he wasn't joking. And Moliere hemorrhaged and collapsed while playing a hypochondriac in one of his own farces. He got up and carried on and then hemorrhaged again and collapsed again and died two hours later.

I myself died in Huddersfield three months ago. Two days later I died in Burnley. Two days after that in Blackpool. People just stopped finding me funny. I stopped finding my*self* funny. Every joke seemed to fall flat and instead of appreciation and love and laughter, it was anger, embarrassment and pity that was coming my way. And finally, and irrevocably, I died three weeks ago in Whitby. It wasn't just that the jokes didn't work. I *froze*. My routine went entirely out of my head. I didn't know what was coming next. I entered this terrible place. This void. The silence just went on and on. And then I just walked off stage.

I remember seeing this amateur performance of *Romeo and Juliet,* about fifteen years ago. The actress playing Juliet forgot her lines and she just stood there, her eyes wide with terror. The fear and humiliation and sense of emptiness were very palpable as the seconds ticked away. I remember thinking that something very real was going on here, something far more authentic, far more interesting than the performance itself. So much more genuine than her performance as Juliet. The real thing.

Laughing Gravy

Fifteen years later there I was. The seconds ticking away. The real thing.

After I walked off stage, I went home to my guest house in Whitby and decided, after tossing and turning in bed for several hours, that me and comedy were through. And that was a great relief I can tell you.

But next morning I came down for breakfast and my landlady asked what would I like - the full English, kippers or porridge? And I couldn't answer. I froze. The fear was still there from the night before. That same terror. I went out without any breakfast and took a walk on the beach to try and calm down. But the terror did not go away. It has not gone away.

That night on stage I did not know what was coming next. The next morning at breakfast I did not know what was coming next. I do not know what is coming next. *You never know what is coming next.*

Smart cookie

Sometimes when somebody is skilful in a sphere of human activity, he or she is described as "a smart cookie." For example, Paul Underwood, who used to live next door to us, emigrated to America, married into money and became Professor of Parapsychology at Beans Island University in Illinois. He was often described by my mother as "a smart cookie."

I have rarely been described as "a smart cookie." When young, I once sat on the branch of a tree in order to saw it in half for firewood. I sat on the wrong side of the branch and, when I had sawn it through, fell to the ground, like in the cartoons, and damaged my head. More recently I was driving on the wrong side of the road and killed a hen. I might have killed the hen had I been driving on the *correct* side of the road but the fact remains that this, and the branch incident, were not the actions of "a smart cookie."

Once or twice, I *have* been described as "a smart cookie." In a recent pub quiz, our team was asked the date of the Battle of Zama. I replied "202 BC." The person who was organizing the quiz said "You are a smart cookie."

But generally, I am not "a smart cookie." In fact, a year ago I did something which wasn't the least bit smart. I sold my soul to the Devil. I was having a bath and the Devil suddenly appeared on the toilet and said he'd buy my soul for £700,000. I instantly agreed and the Devil disappeared. Next day the £700,000 was in my bank account. A lifelong atheist, I have never believed in the existence of a soul. But what if I'm wrong?

On reflection, I don't think selling my soul to the Devil was the action of "a smart cookie."

Macnab is a bitter man

Macnab pulls bitterly on his cigarette and sends a cloud of blue smoke bouncing against the windowpane of his therapist's office. The smoke drifts up to the ceiling where it rests like the aftermath of a minor disaster.

"I'm a bitter man, doctor. And I've got good cause to be bitter. I can tell you that for nothing."

Doctor Clancy has a headache but he tries to appear attentive.

"Why are you bitter Mr. Macnab?"

Macnab gives a harsh, bitter laugh.

"Ha! Why am I bitter? He wants to know why I'm bitter! I'll tell you why I'm bitter!"

But he doesn't. Not immediately. He stares at the long column of ash which is defying gravity at the end of his cigarette.

"You ever been screwed up? So badly it screws up the *rest* of your life?"

As the question appears to be rhetorical, Clancy remains silent.

Macnab taps his chest with a nicotine-stained finger.

"I have! Oh aye, you bet I have!"

"Tell me about it," says Doctor Clancy, who would much rather be on the golf course.

"It was him!" Macnab's face becomes contorted with a poisonous rage. "That swine! Did for me!"

"Who, Mr. Macnab?"

"Doctor Neville Stubbs."

"Doctor...."

"Neville Stubbs. I tracked him down. It wasnae easy. Took me fifty years. You see, it was him that did it. It was him that did it to me."

"Did what?"

"Cut my umbilical cord! That's what! Severed the thing! *Stubbs!* It had been all right up until then. More than all right..."

Macnab smiles sadly.

"I was so happy in the womb. And afterwards. Just lying with Mum. Then he comes along. With his clamps and his big, sterilised scissors. Stubbs!"

Macnab inhales heavily on his cigarette.

"I was going to confront him. I might even have killed him. I was too late. Found out he'd been living in a small Australian mining town near Darwin. But he'd died the previous year."

Macnab removes his flat cap and thrusts his fingers desperately through the strands of silver hair which still cling to his scalp.

"Oh God, it was all downhill since that day. Stubbs and his scissors! And I've tried. Naebody can say I havenae tried..."

"To do what?"

"To get back. To the womb. I've asked her and asked her: "Please mother. Can I come back?""

"And what does she say?"

"You're too big, son."

Macnab replaces his cap.

"She has a point. I admit it."

There is a long silence. Macnab stares out of the window and shakes his head from side to side uncomprehendingly. He is indeed a bitter man.

"I'm a bitter man, doctor. I'm traumatised. What a thing to happen to a helpless wee baby. Why me? That's what I want to know."

"It happens to everybody, Mr. Macnab."

Dr. Clancy's headache is worse. After Macnab has gone, he will cancel his other appointments and drive straight to the golf club.

"It happens to everybody."

But Macnab does not hear.

"I was so happy in the beginning. Why can't life be like it used to be?"

His eyes fill with moisture.

"Why me, doctor? Why me?"

My name is Anguish

Praise for Man Booker prize winning Ludmilla Prism's new novel, "My name is Anguish":

"Prism breathes new life into the detective novel. Detective Inspector Anguish is a marvellous creation. We resonate with his uncertainty, anxiety and forgetfulness. The scene where he turns up to the crime scene without his trousers is simultaneously profoundly comic and profoundly moving."

The Mail on Sunday

"I laughed until I cried. And then I cried until I laughed and then I cried some more. And then I had to lie down and have some hot soup. Prism at the very peak of her prodigious powers."

The Daily Telegraph

"Expands the horizons of what it is to be a human being with a heart, two arms and legs in the 21st Century"

Books and Bookmen

"Ludmilla Prism has it all - wit, elegance, stylishness - and looks. The picture of her on the dust jacket gave me an erection."

The Times Literary Supplement

"By the end of this gut wrenching, magnificent novel I was quite literally coughing up blood. Quite literally the best book of this or any other century."

The Spectator

"In its skilful blend of tragedy and comedy it out Hardy's Hardy and out Wodehouse's Wodehouse. A writer at the top of her game."

The Daily Telegraph

"Monumental. Stunning. Magnificent. Superb. I am a writer who normally eschews superlatives but Prism's novel demands them. The passage where Anguish swallows his mobile phone must stand as one of the most moving in contemporary literature."

Ian Rankin

"I succumbed page after page, lost in wonder at Prism's ability to fix a character or describe a scene with the minimum of words. And what words! Prism uses words the way an expert pastry chef uses pastry. Delicious."

The Guardian

"There are one or two authors working at the coal face of twenty first century literature and producing enormous gold nuggets, gold nuggets of profound significance. Prism is one of those authors. I began this book on a long plane journey from Heathrow to Jakarta. By the time I reached my destination I was so blinded with tears that I could not even see where I was going and fell down the passenger stairs, breaking my thigh bone. It was an injury that was well worth it."

The Herald

"Detective Inspector Bob Anguish and his sidekick, Detective Sergeant Crust, must surely rank alongside Don Quixote and Sancho Panza, and Winnie the Pooh and Piglet, as one of the great literary double acts."

Stephen Fry

"A sinister serial killer, an angst-ridden detective, and an intriguing sub plot involving chlamydia and health insurance. What more can one ask for?"

Empire

"This is a real roller coaster of a novel. In her resistance to cliché and lazy phrasing, Prism is a writer to savour. An absolute page turner."

The Observer

Rejection

Dear Mr. Sarvanend,

Thank you for sending us your novel, *"The Baby Eater."* It is with regret that we inform you that we are unable to publish it at this time. Despite many interesting passages and much light hearted badinage, we feel that it is not the kind of book with which Robson, Bollard and Vum wish to associate themselves. Mr. Bollard was quite adamant that the book would alienate our readership. Unfortunately, books about cannibalistic serial killers are ten a penny these days and although in places your novel had the *joie de vivre* not usually associated with the genre, I believe that the theme is too hackneyed to warrant a further treatment. I may also say that the fact that your manuscript was covered in copious amounts of what looked like thick shred marmalade also argued against our group taking your novel up as a marketable concern.

Sincerely,

Burgo Vum

For Robson, Bollard and Vum.

Dear Mr. Vum,

Thank you for your letter which arrived two months ago but which I am only now replying to due to inertia and mild depression. I understand your reasons for rejecting my novel, *"The Baby Eater."* However, I think you are making a great mistake. This is no ordinary serial killer story. The main character in my novel is a complex and intriguing personality, a man of Messianic intensity and Satanic volitions. He also has a wicked sense of humour. Personally, I believe Eric Cattermole to be the most interesting character to have

Sarvananda

emerged in British literature since Milton's fallen angel appeared on the scene. I beg you to think again.

Sincerely,

Sarvananda.

P.S. The marmalade was not on the manuscript when I sent it. I advise you to ask your colleagues whether some mishap occurred with said manuscript while they were perhaps perusing it over a slapdash breakfast. Please also note spelling of my name.

Dear Mr. Sarvananda,

I apologise for misspelling your name in our letter of rejection. I further apologise for the state of your manuscript. As you rightly surmise, the manuscript was soiled after it was sent to us. Mr. Robson, our senior partner, has many sterling characteristics. Unfortunately, dining room etiquette is not one of them. Indeed, I believe we lost Kingsley Amis's *"Lucky Jim"* to Gollancz due to a mishap involving Mr. Robson and a tin of golden syrup. Nevertheless, our previous criticisms stand and regretfully we are unable to publish your novel, *"The Baby Eater."*

Sincerely,

Burgo Vum

For Robson, Bollard and Vum

P.S. Mr. Robson tells me that the breakfast spread which covers your manuscript was not thick shred marmalade but apricot preserve. Small consolation I know, but it's something.

White Rabbit

I am late for things. I am late for things because too much falls on my head. Consequently, I am constantly threatened with decapitation. Oh yes, take off the head of the White Rabbit! And *then* let's see what would happen to this ludicrous Kingdom. Because nobody else can keep things running.

I was about to say "nobody else can keep things running smoothly" but you can't keep things running smoothly in a madhouse. I won't even say I keep things running *well*. Let's just say I keep things running. And I *am* running from place to place. Always running, anxious, out of breath. But who else around here can provide a bulwark against chaos? Who else has any idea of the workings of Time? The Queen of hearts? Humpty bloody Dumpty? The Mad Hatter? Oh yes, the Mad Hatter! Give the administration and the time management to the Mad Hatter! He and his lunatic friends tried to murder Time. Quite literally. Consequently, it's always tea time over there. Nightmare.

Sometimes, when things get particularly chaotic, when things take on, even more than usual, the shapeless, irrational quality of dreams, I take my pocket watch from my waistcoat, prise open the back and just admire its intricate workings. I gaze in wonder at all those tiny cogs working so well in tandem. I put the watch to my ear and listen to the ticking of the second hand, as regular as clockwork, and am reassured.

One morning my watch stopped. Suddenly I had nowhere to go, nothing to do. And a memory arose of myself as a baby, nibbling dandelions with Mum. The memory was so vivid it was as if I was able to reach out and touch it. It was *present*. And I had this realisation: all Time is present all of the Time. I suddenly felt relieved of a terrible oppression and, do you know, I almost dashed my watch to the ground! But then I remembered the Mad Hatter and just gave it a little tap instead.

And then the watch started up again and I started to run.

Angel Pie

A great hit with my family and a very appropriate dish if a religious dignitary, rabbi, llama or mystic pops round unexpectedly and looks as if he/she might be expecting supper.

You will need:

4 eggs

¼ lb. mushrooms

¼ lb. breadcrumbs

tsp. dill

tsp. rosemary

1 large onion

4 tablespoons angel dust

1 large butterfly net

2 lbs. King Edward potatoes

Method:

Put the potatoes in a big pot and boil, not forgetting the water. When the potatoes are boiled, mash vigorously with a mashing device until potatoes are all fluffy like clouds. Take the eggs and put the inside of the eggs, (the yellow and white parts), into a receptacle and put the shells in the bin. Whisk till all frothy and leave aside. Fry onions until they are brown and smell a bit weird and then add the mushrooms and wait till they're soft. Then bung the whole lot in an oven proof dish along with the bread crumbs which you have already prepared the night before, remembering to keep aside a few tasty morsels for the birds. Now add the dill and rosemary. So far so good. Now find four, quite small angels. For this, you will need to track them down with a big net. You will also need to be able to perceive the angelic presences in the first place. For this, you will need a consciousness which can perceive both literal, scientific truth and the more daimonic reality which resides beneath superficial appearances. Once you have caught the angels, give them a vigorous shake, having first asked their permission. (Being of a magnanimous nature, they are usually happy to oblige.) Catch any dust which falls from the angels' wings in a dish or bowl. Add 4 tablespoonfuls of dust to mix. Release angels into their natural habitat, viz. the Cosmos. Now skilfully aerate the mashed King Edward potato with a fork while whistling quietly and then spread it evenly over the surface of the pie, not forgetting the corners. Place pie in a pre-heated oven at gas number 6. One hour later and, hey presto, your pie will be ready. Consume with a light salad or a stick of rhubarb and using cutlery. Once consumed, you and your guests will almost certainly have visionary experiences. You have also given the angels a good dusting. So, it is a win-win situation for all concerned. Yum yum!

Just in case

Well, yes dear, but you never can be too careful so, just in case, take a hat and scarf. Just in case the weather changes over night. I don't want you catching your death if I'm late. Mrs. Casey was stuck at Edinburgh Waverley for three hours last week, poor soul, waiting for a connection. She was frozen. And she has swollen thighs. No, she had swollen thighs before she got stuck at Waverley. She was attacked by hornets on a Quaker picnic, poor soul. Anyway, keep your mobile to hand just in case I *am* late and need to phone. And obviously you phone me if there are any delays. And take plenty of sandwiches just in case. In fact, best phone the station first thing, before you come out, just in case they cancel your train. I tend to fear the worst, especially with *Virgin*. I like to leave nothing to chance, just in case. Especially with *Virgin*.

I'll see you at the station then, dear. Looking forward to it. Tomorrow. Four o'clock. Yes, I know you know it's four o'clock.... I knew you probably knew. .... Well, just in case you'd forgotten or jotted down the wrong time, dear. I've jotted down the wrong time on more than one occasion myself. And I'm very careful as you know. It's easily done. Oh, and I've bought a couple of wee somethings for you to take back to the kids. A fluffy rabbit for Jane and an Incredible Hulk for Peter. And I've kept the receipt just in case Deirdre doesn't like the fluffy rabbit... Well, because it looks surprisingly fierce for a rabbit. .... Sorry, I certainly *am* bringing an apple pie. I'm bringing one with a sort of wholemeal pastry just in case Lorna's still on that stupid diet.... Well, because nobody should be that thin dear. It's unnatural. I would get her tested just in case it's cancer. .... No, I'm not being morbid. I'm being realistic.

I'll say goodbye now dear just in case my battery runs out. See you at the station. Tomorrow at four o'clock at the station then. Central not General remember.... Yes, I know you probably did but just in case you'd got mixed up. Getting mixed up can happen to the best of us, dear. Oh, and just in case I can't make it tomorrow.... Well, you don't know what tomorrow will bring.... Well, there's this flu thing going around. Mrs. Casey was in an awful state, poor soul.... Yes, she is rather unfortunate health wise. I took her round a flask of soup just in case she needed something hot. Anyway, just in case I inhaled her germs and succumb, or just in case I can't make it tomorrow for whatever reason, I sent that knitting pattern that Lorna wanted through the post. But obviously, I'll let you know if I can't make it. So don't turn off your phone tonight, just in case.

.... Well, I don't think I am, dear. That's a little hurtful. I prefer "careful" to "fussy." *"The best laid schemes of mice and men gang aft a gley."* This is from the mouth of our national bard, dear. And there's a lot of wisdom in those lines. It's certainly been my experience. I mean, it's a constant theme in literature. One of Thomas Hardy's characters pushed a vitally important note under the door and it went straight under the mat and was never received. Hardy really knew his onions. There were dreadful consequences, dear. Hardy knew about life. This chap he wrote about should have double checked, just in case. Sent two notes. Three. Phoned. So *often* things upset the best laid plans. Believe you me. You can't trust anything or anyone, believe you me. So, you need to think of everything. You can never be too careful. Best to leave nothing to chance. Just in case.

Lemons and Lemmings

Daniel Clancy, the founder of the anti-noun movement, was one of the most charismatic speakers I've ever heard. I was at the famous lecture where he first declared war, the lecture which changed so many of our lives, albeit briefly.

"We must wage war on nouns," Clancy declared. "All things are, in reality, process. All is interconnected. We are one another. We are truly equal. There are no boundaries. We must love one another or die. Nouns are sealed pieces of reality. We must knock down their walls and let them melt into the Universe. We are one! We are being! We are life! A noun is a limitation. It is a frozen piece of process. I wage war on nouns!"

And so, he had and he did it so well that for several years nobody knew, to use a rather coarse expression of my father's, "their arse from their elbow."

"There is no self!" Clancy declared in the same lecture. "Another noun! I wage war on the self! Show me this self! Show me where it starts and finishes! We are our parents, our environment, our schooling, our teachers. We are our friends. We are our parents and our parents' parents and we are the vast interplay of forces that shaped our parents and our parents' parents. We are dependant for our existence on sun, moon, tree, one another. There is nothing that is inherently us, inherently me. We are process. This false self, this noun we construct, is a closet of fear. We must burst open the door of that closet and welcome life, embrace the Universe. I demand the removal of all labels - no man, no woman, no black, no white, - no self! I announce the death of the self!"

Clancy was persuasive. There was no doubt of that. Within a month of his speech, anti-noun workshops had spread all over the country. We used to wander around the room pointing at things and giving them the wrong names – (although Clancy said that there were no "wrong" names.) "Cat," we would say, pointing at the door; "apple," pointing at someone's hat; "margarine," pointing at a plate; "hamster", pointing at a table. They were hilarious games - at first.

Then we had workshops where men would become women for a day and women, men; workshops where the aristocracy would lead working class lifestyles for a week and vice versa. We even had a workshop where we were asked to bring our pets and they ended up leading the workshop.

But very soon it began to get silly. People's vocabulary started breaking down. People began to stop understanding one another.

I ordered a salad at my favourite vegetarian restaurant and got squid. My nephew's GP prescribed haemorrhoid cream for his acne. An old woman stopped me in the street one afternoon, grabbed my arm and told me that she thought she was losing her melon. I told her I thought I knew what she meant but wasn't sure.

It was not long before Clancy went totally insane, although his disciples refused to accept the fact, declaring that Clancy was challenging self-view and reification. I remember wandering into a pub in Great Western Road and seeing Clancy's face, pinched and gaunt, haunted and staring.... He was surrounded by a throng of admiring disciples.

"Could someone tell me my god-damn name?" yelled Clancy.

His disciples laughed.

"I mean it man! What's my name?" Clancy was screaming.

"Tomato," said one disciple.

"Calculator bones," said another.

"Fudge sundae," said a third.

Society was going to hell. Trade Unions were demanding wage cuts for their members. The elderly were being herded into nurseries and infants were being admitted into care homes. People squeezed lemmings into their salads and put lemons in zoos.

The counter revolution was sudden and successful. Spearheaded by a bank clerk from Colchester, a Mr. Morris Thing, and united under the banner "Back the British Noun", sanity was promptly restored. Where Clancy was charismatic, Thing was ponderous, long-winded, and dull – but utterly popular. In a three-hour broadcast to the nation Morris Thing took item after item from an array of bags and suitcases and explained each item's meaning and function.

"This is a pen," he would say in that monotonous nasal voice, holding a pen up to the camera. "It is my pen. It is not your pen. I bought this pen with my money. It is not an elephant. It is not a sideboard. It is not a dog, a pomegranate, or a piece of Battenburg cake. It is a pen. It is my pen. I bought it with my money."

The programme was watched with relief in millions of homes across the country. The brief assault on the noun was over.

I too felt that same sense of relief. I was on *terra firma* again. After the broadcast I took a long walk and savoured the sound of what were very definitely my feet on the reassuringly hard and steadfast pavement.

But, as I walked through the suburbs, passed all the large, lonely houses, glimpsed all the families sitting in their living rooms watching the flickering screens of their television sets, I also realised that something hugely important may have been irrevocably lost.

Improve your breakfast

Have you noticed how dull breakfasts have become? I certainly have.

In the old days, when God existed, you'd say grace before every meal and, as you munched happily at your toast, you'd feel secure and happy in the scheme of things and your breakfast would be invested with the Lord's presence. Now, with the death of God, this is no longer possible and breakfasts now reflect the contemporary, flavourless *zeitgeist*.

However, there is a solution. Celebrities have filled the gap where God used to be and our devotion is now directed towards them. So, all you have to do, in order to reinvest your breakfast with flavour and meaning, is to have breakfast with a celebrity.

Imagine. You are seated at your breakfast bar struggling through a plate of Bran Flakes and soya milk. Suddenly Sofia Coppola, American film-maker, and star of hit movies such as *Godfather III,* enters. Sofia Coppola is the daughter of celebrated and multi award winning movie director, Francis Ford Coppola, and she's also the cousin of famous actors, Nicolas Cage and Jason Schwartzman, so in a sense, a whole movie dynasty has entered your kitchen. Sofia Coppola sits down beside you at your breakfast bar and you give her a plate of Bran Flakes. The two of you munch away and you ask Sofia what she's been up to lately. She tells you. Perhaps she's been making a block-busting movie or writing her memoirs. Perhaps she's been attending a charity gala or been to an awards ceremony. Perhaps she's been rubbing shoulders with other celebrities or taking it easy at home with her famous husband, Thomas Mars, lead singer of the indie pop band, *Phoenix*. Whatever Sofia's been doing, it's bound to have been interesting

Laughing Gravy

After Sofia leaves, you suddenly notice that your breakfast has never tasted quite so good and, in the days, weeks and months to come, you recall Sofia's early morning visit and consume your breakfast with a tranquil smile.

Your life now has purpose.

The Tourist's Guide to Hell

Introduction

From lakes of fire to freezing black pits, Hell offers the traveler an experience of extreme and enthralling contrasts. Being a location of such extremes, it is often quite tricky to decide on the appropriate clothing. But necessities should include sun cream with a very high block factor and a woolly nose cup to counteract frostbite.

A place of astonishing mediocrity and sublime banality, time passes very slowly here and so it's possible to see all the sites in a single morning, leaving the rest of the time for self-recrimination, boredom and finding fault with your fellow traveler. For although Hell is sometimes best enjoyed in complete isolation, to fully savour its riches, it is sometimes best to go with a companion – for example, an ex-lover or spouse with whom you have recently and acrimoniously split up; or an aggravating parent.

Travelers to Hell often experience high levels of anxiety so mindfulness is the watchword at all times. When walking through Hell, (public transport is very unreliable), it is advised to constantly bring your attention back to the breath and the soles of the feet. It is also advised to avoid eye contact with the locals.

Places to go and things to do

Brimstone Lake

Boat trips three times a day. Fishing is permitted but entirely fruitless.

The Pit of Damnation

Laughing Gravy

It is a long climb up Mount Vile but the view from the top of the mountain into the pit of Hell itself is well worth the effort. It is a popular destination for tourists with troublesome relatives.

Triple XXX Night Club

Hell's hottest night spot boasts the boiling Jacuzzi, the self-flagellation room, regular orgies involving the animal of your choice and many other attractions designed to fully satisfy the visitor bent on self-abasement.

Museum of Complete Bastards

Famous exhibits include Lizzie Borden's original axe, Hitler's moustache, Mao Tse Tung's chopsticks and Ivan the Terrible's coasters. At three pm every day there is an animated film for children - *The Funny World of Vlad the Impaler*. The kids might also like to play with the artifacts and tease Mum and Dad in the hands-on Spanish Inquisition Room. For an extra 25 Kronen you can also try *The Josef Stalin Experience*, a simulated recreation of 1930's Russia which includes the Beria Room where you can be tortured in relative comfort, the Show Trial Room where you and your friends can be condemned to death on trumped up charges, and the Siberia Room. (Warm clothing a necessity!)

La Scala Cinema

The La Scala has been showing the same two films for a number of years now. In the afternoon you can catch the 1973 Reg Varney vehicle, *Holiday on the Buses* and in the evening there are regular showings of *Titanic,* a teen romance set on board a big ship.

The Jean Paul Sartre Bar and Bistro

*"*Hell is other people,*"* stated the famous French philosopher and the Jean Paul Sartre Bar and Bistro, which occupies three floors, boasts some of the most opinionated, boring, self-pitying, and uninteresting people you are ever likely to meet. Local character, David Slyme, is constantly on hand to

display his collection of beer mats, acquired over several decades. Mein host, Colonel Harry Barbary-Waring, is a racist and homophobe and will deny entry to anyone he suspects of belonging to a minority group. Live music is provided on the second floor by *The Showaddywaddy Tribute Band*, and entertainment is also provided by ex-members of the 60's and 70's UK dance troupe, *the Younger Generation,* (now reformed as *The Pastel Shades*). For an extra 30 Kronen you can get trapped in the lift with a Jehovah's witness.

The Guilt Trip

A circular tour of all of Hell's tourist spots accompanied by a Church of Scotland minister or a Catholic priest (depending on your denomination.)

Where to stay

Dunroamin Guest House, Brimstone Road.

Centrally situated in Hell's main tourist thoroughfare, Dunroamin Guest House has been a regular haven for travelers for over thirty years. The proprietress, Mrs. Irene MacDougall, is a bitter alcoholic and is renowned for making all guests extremely unwelcome. Her breakfasts are almost impossible to hold down, the general level of service is appalling and the Seventies décor, (including the chocolatey-orange geometrically designed wallpaper in the residents' lounge) has been known to provoke severe bouts of mental illness. Dunroamin is conveniently placed for the local Vomitorium.

Beelzebub Bed and Breakfast, Beelzebub Street.

Sarcastic, morose and with little or no personal hygiene to speak of, proprietors Paula and George Ferris, will make your stay here quite exceptionally harrowing. Every room has an *en suite* shower which is either too hot or too cold, a faulty table lamp which will electrocute the unwary, and damp, moss encrusted linen. Paula's mother, Mrs. Edna Stewart, will constantly attempt to borrow money from you. Don't give her any as it fuels her glue sniffing habit. Avoid the soup of the day.

Hell YMCA. Satan Street.

One dormitory with five hundred beds. One leaky gas stove. One chemical toilet.

Note

Finally, as with any holiday destination, the mental state with which you embark upon your visit is very important. In this regard, to fully relish Hell, it's advisable to abandon all hope.

Anorak

Last night saw another addition to the pantheon of Scandinavian *noir* detectives in the shape of Finnish Chief Inspector, Jarmo Anorak. In last night's episode, we see Anorak buying some fish at the local market. Then, after purchasing a bottle of wine, he drives over to his sister's house. Here, brother and sister cook together, and share a meal. As they're finishing the fish course, Anorak's superior, Chief of Police, Ari Friedlander, phones Anorak to say that there has been a vicious murder at the docks and will Anorak go over and investigate. Anorak says he's unable to do this as he never works weekends and they haven't had pudding yet. The episode finishes with Anorak, his sister and his sister's son, Perti, playing *Scrabble,* chatting and watching some television over coffee and cake.

Anorak's unusual for a screen detective in that he has no evident personal problems, apart from his asthma which he manages well with an inhaler. He's psychologically well-adjusted and only has one glass of wine over dinner. If it's tense and visceral drama you're after, then *Anorak* will prove a disappointment. In fact, there's no tension at all in this first episode apart from a brief two minutes of suspense when Anorak mislays his car keys. There are no bloody murders, no red herrings, (the fish that Anorak and his sister cook is cod), and no mysterious serial killer who leaves clues at the crime scene. There is no whodunnit element, (although one briefly suspects somebody of hiding Anorak's car keys in the fruit bowl), no wise- cracking assistant and no authoritarian boss. In fact, Chief of Police, Ari Friedlander, is very understanding about Anorak's refusal to work weekends.

All this will put many people off the series.

I myself found it remarkably soothing.

Creosote

Mrs. Angel was sharing her reflections on human sensuality with the other residents of her care home. (Mind you, apart from Mrs. Gold, the other residents were asleep. Or pretending to be.)

"I find it very interesting," Mrs. Angel was saying, "that when someone wants your undivided attention, they will say, 'listen to me!' or 'look at me!' but never '*smell* me!'"

"I should hope not," said Mrs. Gold. "As an ex-schoolteacher, I can say categorically that I wouldn't have wanted my pupils *sniffing* me."

"Why not?"

"To permit someone access to one's bodily aromas, particularly to use the imperative in that regard, seems beyond the pale, Betty. I doubt if I even granted the late Mr. Gold that level of intimacy."

"But don't you wish," said Mrs. Angel, "that our sense of smell was more developed?"

"Possibly," conceded Mrs. Gold.

"Don't you envy our canine sisters and brothers?" Mrs. Angel persisted enthusiastically. "I do wish I'd been born a dog with a vast olfactory vocabulary at my disposal."

"Well, *you* may wish to spend your day smelling other people's bottoms Betty," said Mrs. Gold, "but it's certainly not *my* cup of tea."

"I've always had a well-developed sense of smell," said Mrs. Angel. "Do you know, Janet, that the merest whiff of creosote transports me back to childhood?" She smiled happily. "Every summer Daddy and I would be out there with those big brushes, preserving the fence…"

"Terrible word, '*creosote,*'" said Mrs. Gold, shuddering.

(Mrs. Gold was a bit of a poet, truth be told.)

"I can even smell death you know," said Mrs. Angel, looking significantly at Mrs. Baird who was snoring gently in her wheelchair on the opposite side of the lounge.

Sure enough, Mrs. Baird died in her sleep that night.

After that, when she was talking to Mrs. Angel, Mrs. Gold made sure she was sitting next to an open window.

Infestation

I found a fairy in my wheelie bin two weeks ago. I'm not talking about one of my gay mates who might have been having a kip in there after a heavy night at *Sizzlers*. This fairy was a transparent being with gossamer wings. And he - or she – or whatever gender you might want to assign the thing - was not the only fairy I found that day. In fact, I soon realised that the bloody things had infested the entire house and garden. Fairies. And these weren't the scary fairies of old, the no-nonsense Celtic fairies who stole your kids away and scared the living hell out of you. No, the fairies who'd infested my house and garden were the little sprite-like things out of Victorian illustrations. They were light green in colour, always smiling, and had little flowery caps. They were the sentimental, syrupy sort of fairy and, frankly, I didn't like them.

They were everywhere: behind the skirting board, under the sink, in the garden shed, in the shrubbery, behind the bookshelves... I even found one shivering in the fridge.

They kept me awake. I heard them at night, under the floorboards, their little wings and taffeta skirts *rustling*. And sometimes I could hear them singing these sugary sweet little songs. Their songs made me feel nauseous, as if I'd been eating too much chocolate. Fairy Muzak. Horrible. Bloody sickly fairies everywhere. And their bloody sickly singing.

So, I went on the net and I found a Fairy Exterminator and rang him but he turned out to be some awful Evangelical Christian homophobe so I gave him short shrift. And then I discovered this other bloke on the net and he came over to have a sniff around. His name was Adrian De Vere and he looked like he'd stepped out of Dickens. He wore a velvet smoking jacket and a little tasselled cap and he had enormous side whiskers and he looked around the house and he said, "Yes, you've got fairies."

And I said, "I know I've got fairies. Can you get rid of them?"

And Adrian de Vere said that yes, he probably could, but they weren't like rats, you couldn't just put out poison for them and what I needed to do was engage them in conversation because the fairies were sustained by my particular belief system, and I said how could that possibly be true as I was a scientific materialist and believed solely in the power of reason and I didn't believe in fairies and never had, and Adrian de Vere said, "Well, they're everywhere sir, and I presume you can't deny the evidence of your own eyes and you're not, I presume, insane sir, so I'm afraid that in some corner of your psyche you have a belief in the Victorian style of fairy and if you want to rid your house and garden of the wee creatures, then you must fully acknowledge that fact."

Well, I bridled at all this and suggested that the fairies might have come from Mrs. Constable's next door as she was very old and dotty and wrote to the local paper about UFOs. But Adrian de Vere said that many scientific materialists like myself can be overly rational and a bit cynical and that the fairies were almost certainly an extreme compensation mechanism which had kicked in as a sentimental reaction to the one-sided nature of my personality. All I had to do, suggested Adrian de Vere, was to say to the fairies – (individually, which might take some time) – "I love you. I believe in you." And then they might decamp.

After Adrian de Vere had gone, I had a stiff whisky and contemplated what he'd been saying. Perhaps, I concluded, there *was* a side of me which wished to experience a more non-rational aspect of Reality, an aspect which opened the heart to a world of myth. So, after another whisky, I began to go around the house addressing the fairies one by one and saying that I loved them and believed in them. Initially I felt self-conscious, irritable and embarrassed but the effects of the whisky soon began to make me feel maudlin and I began to actually believe that I believed in the little sprites. And, as my conviction grew, the fairies began to fade – and finally, one after another, to disappear. By the end of that day there wasn't a single fairy in my house, shed, conservatory, or garden.

Trouble is, I've started to miss them.

The raising of Lazarus

Paw Broon was glad that he'd ordered an extra barrel of beer. A lot of drink had been downed that night.

They'd done Lazarus proud. He would have enjoyed the evening himself, that was for sure.

Paw, seated in his old armchair by the blazing fire, was feeling sad but mellow. He peered through the curtain of fag smoke at his brother's coffin which stood on a wobbly trestle table and was bedecked with beer bottles, ash trays and wine glasses. Paw smiled. A fair drinker, the same man. And he'd smoked like a lum. It had all done for him in the end but not before he'd had a good old innings. And they'd remembered him with songs, laughter and tears. Aye, they'd given him a good send off. It had been a fine evening.

The Mackenzie brothers, their arms around one another's shoulders, were swaying slowly from side to side to the accordion music. Annie, Lazarus's widow, was dead drunk, sat at the pantry table with her head resting on her folded arms. The twins lay curled up on the sofa. It was getting late. Paw sighed and began to heave himself out of the armchair. He was getting too old for all this carry on. And it was the man's funeral tomorrow.

It was then that the pantry door opened and a chill wind blew into the room. A man entered, a tall man dressed entirely in white with wide, staring eyes and an expression on his face which would turn milk quite sour.

The accordion stopped playing. There was a hush as the frosty presence looked around at the assembly. He gave a stiff smile. It was like ice cracking on the surface of a pond.

"Please," he said, "carry on."

Paw knew the man and disliked him as an interfering busybody. His name was Jesus, a minister from a neighbouring parish, a man awkward in company who would never take a dram. He was a silent and subdued fellow but, like all the worst ministers, full of a passionate intensity when he got into the pulpit.

"Would you like a drink, Minister?" asked Paw. "An Iron Brew?"

"No. Thank you. No."

He spoke so softly that Paw had to strain to hear what he was saying.

"A crisp then?" asked Maw.

"Thank you, no."

Jesus, Paw noted, was eyeing the coffin and there was a harsh gleam in his eye.

"I'll just sit here, Mr. Broon."

Jesus sat on the little chair by the coffin with his hands in his lap, looking around at the assembly with a stiff smile which did nothing to disguise his customary disapproval.

The accordion started up again but there was no feeling or life in the melody.

Conversation was stilted and subdued.

Suddenly Jesus got to his feet and swept the beer bottles, ash trays, wine glasses and bowls of crisps from the lid of the coffin. The music immediately stopped. Paw's heart began to hammer in his chest.

"Lazarus," announced Jesus loudly, "was a fine man. And I know his mission on earth was not finished! Hand me a screwdriver!"

Nobody moved. Nobody spoke.

"I need," commanded Jesus, "a screwdriver!"

And Daphne, trembling at the terrible authority of the man, went and fetched a screwdriver from the kitchen cupboard.

It took a while for Jesus to remove the screws from the lid of the coffin. His intense excitement had made his hands shake. Finally however, he removed the lid and placed it against the parlour wall.

"Now then, Minister," said Paw, touching Jesus's arm lightly with his hand. "Come on now."

For Paw had seen the harsh gleam in the minister's eyes become a mad, messianic stare.

"Leave him alane, Minister," said Hen, who was afraid that the man might kiss Uncle Lazarus. Or something even more distasteful. (They'd decided on a closed coffin for a reason. The cancer had been very advanced.)

"He's laid to rest," went on Hen. "Dinnae disturb him."

"Oh, ye of little faith!" cried Jesus, sending little stars of spittle over the assembled company.

He was like that, considered Paw. Frowning and silent most of the time and then suddenly histrionic.

Gently Jesus placed his hands on the cold, waxen and emaciated face that stared sightlessly up at him.

"Arise Lazarus!" cried Jesus. "Arise!"

"Stop that nonsense, Minister!" cried Maw Broon, her face ashen. "Stop him someone!"

But everyone was rooted to the spot.

Jesus's body was shaking. He looked upwards and gave a kind of snarling scream.

"Oh, my Father in Heaven! Raise thy servant, Lazarus!"

The body stirred.

Uncle Lazarus, very slowly, very stiffly, sat up in the coffin. His face was harrowed, gaunt and yellow-white, the colour of old newspapers. His best suit hung ridiculously from his emaciated frame and his bowler hat was clutched violently to his chest between skeletal hands.

Laughing Gravy

For a few, terrible seconds nobody moved.

"Whit the bloody hell's goin oan here, Paw?" Lazarus asked his brother.

And then the spell was broken. There was a screaming and a shrieking as everybody made for the door, crashing into one another as they scrambled out of the pantry. You could hear their cries slowly receding down Glebe Street until finally there was silence. Leaving Paw, Jesus and Lazarus - who was staring in complete bewilderment at his benefactor.

"Farewell my good and faithful servant," said Jesus.

He patted Lazarus on the head, smiled, and then strode purposefully out of the open door.

Paw sat down heavily on the little chair which Jesus had just vacated. He sighed and looked dejectedly at his brother.

"You hungry? You want a sandwich or something? How are you feeling?"

"Bloody terrible," said Lazarus. "Like death warmed up."

"You're not looking very bonny," admitted Paw.

He put his chin mournfully in his hands as Lazarus continued to stare in confusion around the room.

"Still, it's good to have you back," said Paw. He looked at the horribly wasted form of his brother. "I suppose...."

An eyeball dropped from Lazarus's eye socket into his lap.

It was all, reflected Paw, going to be a bit of a problem.

Prime numbers

For Jackie Cannon

"Three, five, seven, eleven, thirteen," said Mr. Trellis.

"I refuse to be drawn," said Mrs. Gaberdine.

"Seventeen, nineteen, twenty-three," he went on.

He was smiling. He seemed happy.

"Twenty-nine, thirty-one, thirty-seven, forty-three." He paused to consider. "Forty-seven."

"I'm not intimidated by this behaviour," said Mrs. Gaberdine.

"Fifty-three. Fifty-seven."

"Fifty-seven?" asked Mrs. Gaberdine softly.

Mr. Trellis looked momentarily discomfited. "Sorry. Not fifty-seven. Fifty-nine. Sixty-one," he proceeded. "Sixty-seven. Seventy-one."

As he recited the numbers, he washed the plates with a more than necessary thoroughness. With a certain ironic zest.

"Seventy-three," he said.

Mrs. Gaberdine was upset. She left Mr. Trellis with the dishes, went into the living room, and sat in front of the TV. After a while, she heard the hum of the vacuum cleaner. Mr. Trellis didn't normally vacuum. In fact, Mrs. Gaberdine couldn't remember the last time her lodger had done any vacuuming. She wondered if Mr. Trellis was still reciting numbers while he vacuumed. The last time he'd recited numbers, it had gone on for two whole days.

Mrs. Gaberdine couldn't help herself. She wandered into the hall where, sure enough, Mr. Trellis was gleefully chanting as he pressed the vacuum attachment into the corners of the hall carpet.

"Two hundred and seventy-one," he said. "Two hundred and seventy-seven...."

"Mr. Trellis is reciting prime numbers," Mrs. Gaberdine told Robert, her therapist, the next day. Mrs. Gaberdine had been going to see Robert for some time, initially to remove a minor spider neurosis, and she had very much enjoyed her sessions. But Robert had recently started talking of "closure." Mrs. Gaberdine had to admit (to herself) that she probably didn't need therapy any more - but she was a shy woman and the chance to talk about herself at length didn't present itself in any other context. And Robert was such a nice man, even if his taste in cardigans was a bit dubious. So, she had persuaded Robert to let her continue until the end of the year, although recently she'd been struggling to find a problem or neurosis to explore with him. Today however, the problem of Mr Trellis, though not strictly psychological, was at the forefront of her mind.

"He sometimes gets it wrong, Robert. But that's what he's up to. Reciting prime numbers"

"Why's he doing that?"

"I think it might be some kind of veiled criticism."

"How do you mean?"

"Well, his last funny turn occurred last month. He started wearing my earrings to breakfast and when I tried to talk to him, he just started reciting numbers. Prime numbers. Like he's doing now."

"How was that a 'veiled criticism', as you put it?"

"Well, the previous morning at breakfast, he'd been picking lumps of wax out of his ears and placing them on the table cloth and I said 'Mr. Trellis, that's not very nice. You should get your ears syringed.'"

"What did he say to that?"

"'Pardon?'"

"What did he say to that?"

"No, that's what he said. 'Pardon?' Pretended not to hear. And next morning came down to breakfast wearing my earrings and reciting prime numbers."

"Hmm. Why such odd behaviour? Why couldn't he just have said, 'Please don't make personal comments about my ear wax?'"

"Mr. Trellis is a bit tangential, Robert. He's not at all straight forward." Mrs. Gaberdine sighed.

"So, what do you think brought on yesterday's episode?"

"I was spring cleaning and I went into Mr. Trellis's room and I said, 'What a mess, Mr. Trellis. This room needs a good dusting.' He didn't say anything but after dinner, he put on my apron and started washing the dishes and vacuuming and reciting prime numbers."

Mrs. Gaberdine realised she felt very upset at her lodger's behaviour. She had felt close to tears as she'd recounted Mr. Trellis's extraordinary behaviour to Robert.

Robert was leaning back in his chair staring at the ceiling. Mrs. Gaberdine hoped he wouldn't overbalance. It had happened before.

"What *is* a prime number, Mrs. Gaberdine?" asked Robert.

"Well, it's a number which is indivisible by any other number. Three's a prime number. Five. Seven, and so on."

"Precisely. A prime number is indivisible. It won't be changed by any other number. It has a quality of independence, even unreasonableness about it. Thirty-seven. Defiant. Independent. Not to be argued with - or reasoned with under any circumstances"

"I don't follow, Robert. What has this to do with Mr. Trellis?"

Robert leant forward and smiled. (Somewhat patronizingly, Mrs Gaberdine thought.)

"I just wonder, Mrs. Gaberdine, if Mr Trellis is trying to make a point. You are quite an orderly woman. Rational. Reasonable. Perhaps even a little unsurprising…."

Mrs. Gaberdine felt a surge of irritability - but nodded, not wanting to hurt Robert's feelings.

"I suspect your lodger is trying to assert his independence. He is perhaps asserting his refusal to be constrained by your reason or orderliness or desire for control… Your Mr. Trellis is a prime number, I suspect. He prizes his spontaneity and irrationality. He won't be argued with or changed!"

"But what should I do?"

"Does he recite the prime numbers sequentially or at random?" asked Robert.

"Sequentially."

"In that case, ignore him. He'll soon run out of steam."

When Mrs. Gaberdine got in that afternoon, Mr. Trellis, still wearing an apron, was vigorously dusting the television set.

"Thirty-five thousand, seven hundred and forty-nine," he said.

He looked tired. There were bags under his eyes.

Mrs. Gaberdine took a deep breath and smiled.

"Afternoon Mr. Trellis," she said. "How are we?"

"Thirty-five thousand, seven hundred and fifty-three."

Mrs. Gaberdine pondered. He was probably right. It didn't divide by three, seven or nine for a start....

"Thirty-five thousand, seven hundred and seventy-one."

But Mrs. Gaberdine ignored him and switched on the television.

"Gets more difficult as you go on, "said Mr. Trellis. He suddenly sat down in the middle of the floor. "I think I'll stop now."

Sarvananda

For a few months, Mr. Trellis was an exemplary tenant. He displayed some minor eccentricities, it's true, but Mrs. Gaberdine found such eccentricities tolerable, unlike the extremely disturbing behaviour which she had witnessed of late. Then one day, Mr. Trellis was washing the outside windows. He had seemed quite helpful recently and Mrs. Gaberdine had wondered if it was because he'd been a bit ashamed of his recent behaviour and had wanted to make it up to her. She felt that perhaps Mr. Trellis had turned over a new leaf.

Unfortunately, it was not to be. Mrs. Gaberdine was dead-heading the roses when she looked up to observe Mr. Trellis leaning precariously over the very top of the ladder as he attempted to reach the corner of the attic window with his sponge.

"For goodness's sake, be careful Mr. Trellis!" Mrs. Gaberdine called up to him. "You could have an accident!"

Mr. Trellis's hand froze.

"Three," he said. "Five. Seven..."

Mrs. Gaberdine hurried into the house, changed out of her gardening clothes, and walked into the town.

She could hardly bring herself to return home. What, she wondered, as she sipped her third coffee in succession at *Latte Central*, would the wretched man be up to now? That is, if he was still alive.

In fact, when she got home, she found her lodger walking on the top of the roof, balancing on the ridge tiles, and still reciting prime numbers at the top of his voice. Mrs. Gaberdine attempted to ignore him, knowing that any admonition would make things worse, and went inside to make her supper.

For the next hour… two hours… three hours…. Mrs. Gaberdine could hear Mr Trellis striding to and fro on the roof and reciting his numbers in that hugely irritating monotone.

Laughing Gravy

Finally, she couldn't stand it any longer and went outside to plead with her lodger to come in.

"Mr. Trellis, please come down! It's getting dark!"

But he didn't come down. For a long time Mrs. Gaberdine stared up at the figure which was disappearing into the twilight - and then she went inside and had a bubble bath.

Next morning Mrs Gaberdine woke very early after a disturbed night and came downstairs to hear prime numbers emerging from the fireplace in the living room. Mr. Trellis was still up there. Wearily, Mrs. Gaberdine went outside into the grey dawn and looked up at her lodger walking slowly along the rooftop and shouting his numbers into the nondescript morning sky.

And then a devilish feeling began to form in Mrs. Gaberdine's breast. A phrase crystallised in her mind.

What made her shout it out? Had she just had enough of her lodger? Was it the fact that she had felt stung at Robert's description of her as "unsurprising" and "rational"? Because surely, she knew that Mr Trellis would react, would *have* to react, to any admonition, however minor. It was in his nature.

Anyway, this is what she yelled up at him:

"For God's sake be careful, Mr. Trellis! That is just not acceptable behaviour! You'll have a terrible accident!"

Mr. Trellis stopped walking along the ridge of the roof. Then slowly, very slowly, he began to perform a handstand. At the same time his recitation of prime numbers speeded up. And for a full three minutes Mr Trellis, quite heroically some might say, remained in that position. Before overbalancing.

Mrs. Gaberdine would say to herself in the months and years to come that she hadn't done anything wrong. She had just said what anyone would have said, given the circumstances. But sometimes, especially when she was dusting or cleaning, she remembered that strange, devilish desire in her breast, a desire that Robert might have called "irrational" or "surprising" - and felt a terrible sense of guilt.

And from that day forth, she could never see a prime number or hear one recited in company without envisaging a small man in house slippers and corduroy trousers plummeting to his death from the roof of her house.

Plays and monologues

Of the plays and monologues included in this section, *Superhero; A short lecture on comedy; Concluding remarks* and *Angulimala: portrait of a serial killer* were all written for performance at Buddhist festivals. In *Angulimala*, I played the title character, the part of Angulimala's Mum was played by Satyadaka and Sam Wilkin played the Buddha. I originally performed *Death: a case for the defence* at the Paranirvana festival at Norwich Buddhist Centre, about a month before Covid kicked off. (I very much enjoyed playing Death as an old tramp in dark, nasty suit, grotty old cardigan, fingerless gloves and crumpled and dusty bowler hat.) I adapted the play for radio, updating it to make mention of Covid, but the BBC didn't take to it. It's this untransmitted radio version that I've included here.

Family Values and *A short sermon* were written for my own amusement and have never been performed. *Family values* is the oldest (and silliest) of the plays included, written in those happy days when there were no mobile phones and the Queen Mother was still alive. Church of Scotland ministers figure a lot in my writing and *A short sermon* is my revenge upon those religious dignitaries who subjected me to hour upon hour of excruciating boredom as a boy. It does not reflect upon the two kind and intelligent men who were the ministers in my home parish in Glasgow.

Any of these plays and monologues can be performed with my permission. *Angulimala* was performed with Glasgow accents but you may substitute the dialect of your choice. Angulimala's Mum plays a saxophone at the end of the play but you may wish to use another instrument or, if unmusical, incorporate any suitably ridiculous hobby.

A short lecture on comedy

(**Doctor Nigel Spalding**, *a noted academic and Buddhist practitioner, comes to the podium. He is very nervous, which he tries to hide by relying on his notes and his academic persona. When he does look up from his notes or tries to ad lib, he becomes confused or embarrassed.*)

Doctor Spalding: Fellow spiritual aspirants... When I was asked to give a short talk on the fiftieth anniversary of our Buddhist Order, I was initially unsure as to what form such a talk might take. As an academic, I was unsure how appropriate any primarily *intellectual* stimuli might be on an occasion such as this. However, in keeping with the celebratory nature of this festival, I have decided to give a brief lecture on the subject of comedy. And hopefully, in this short talk, I can both incorporate a sense of festive holiday spirit - *and* make links between comedy and the Buddhist way of life with particular reference to the Dharma of our own teacher, Sangharakshita. (By the way, for those of you who are particularly interested in the *political* nature of my theme, I refer you to my recent paper on comedy and politics, published by Oxford University Press, entitled *Karl and Groucho Marx: some affinities.*)

So. Firstly I think we need to define our terms. What is comedy? What indeed *is* comedy? I confess I'm not very sure. The Greek dramatist and comic playwright, Aristophanes, when asked this question, retorted with a witty jest. He said *"Mi me rotas. Eimai menu lithoxous"*. That is - *"Don't ask me, I'm only a stone mason."* (Slight laugh.) Aristophanes was using a complex play on words here and possibly referring to one of his previous occupations and the joke does not translate that well from the Ancient Greek. Obviously. But the point is made. Whether we find

Laughing Gravy

Aristophanes' original joke humorous or not, and many of us here tonight did *not*, the point is a salient one. Aristophanes refused to define comedy. And I too tonight want to begin to do just that. Begin to refuse to define comedy. Nevertheless, I think a few *tentative* definitions are permissible.

So, to help us in this respect, I'd like to look at Sangharakshita's seminal work *The Religion of Art,* published almost fifty years ago and yet still very relevant. In *The Religion of Art* Sangharakshita famously defined art thus: *"Art is the organisation of sensuous impressions into pleasurable formal relations that express the artist's sensibility and communicate to his audience a sense of values that can transform their lives."* Now if we change but three words here; the first, the eleventh and the seventeenth, we have the following: *"COMEDY is the organisation of sensuous impressions into FUNNY formal relations that express the COMEDIAN'S sensibility and communicate to his audience a sense of values that can transform their lives."* So, by changing but three words, we have a radically new definition *of*, and a radically new perspective *on,* comedy. So, whenever we give or receive humour, jokes, badinage, repartee, let us bear this definition in mind. Before you laugh just reflect on Sangharakshita's definition - with the three minor adjustments I have made. If indeed the joke or amusing anecdote *has* communicated to you a sense of values that you believe will change your life, then laugh. If the joke has failed in this vital respect, then it is probably better to with-hold your laughter.

Incidentally, Sangharakshita has often referred to the poet Keats and his theory of negative capability. By which Keats means the ability to live and create in uncertainty. Without certainties, without the need to control, without dogma of any kind. Comedy too, in its dislike of certainties and dogma, points us towards uncertainty and *(Pause as he turns over one of his note cards)* spontaneity.

Let us now look at another aspect of comedy. Comedy and phallus worship. Comedy has its roots in the ancient goat songs, in the phallic songs, in phallus worship. Thus, the comic has always had its roots in the *(He is not at all relaxed about being sexually explicit)* erect penis. And thus, comedy celebrates the life force: energy, vitality, sexual potency. So, comedy is always sowing the seeds of new life. Impregnating. Entering. Ejaculating. Thrusting. *(Gives a rather embarrassed, half-hearted gesture with his arm.)* So to speak. Yes. Um. And thus, comedy celebrates the life force: potency, sexual potency. As I may have just said. We can still see this reflected in our modern clowns: Charlie Chaplin and his cane, Ken Dodd and his tickling stick, Les Patterson and his huge, unruly member. So, comedy is always sowing the seeds of new life. The comic muse is no sweet, virginal youth but a monstrous satyr who, with erect member, seeks always to undermine our bourgeois certainties with his antics, escapades and ballocks. Sorry, frolics. He seeks to sow his seed in the corresponding.... I think I'll curtail this a little and move on due to time restraints.

Moving on now to a *philosophical* take on comedy, let us take a look at what Henri Bergson had to say about comedy. Comedy, Bergson suggests, addresses our habitual, mechanical and repetitive behaviour. Bergson argues that we laugh, as it were correctively, as a matter of vigilance, on behalf of our creative intuition that a really living life should never repeat itself. Let me say that again. We laugh, as it were correctively, as a matter of vigilance, on behalf of our creative intuition that a really living life should never repeat itself. Laughter then, in Bergson's view, is a release of energy, the energy suppressed in mechanical, habitual behaviour. It simultaneously destroys the habitual and repetitive. And challenges the ego. Bergson gives the example of.... gives the example of.... *(Spalding has lost some of his notes)*. a lecturer who... ironically enough.... loses some of his lecture notes and has to improvise.... *(He becomes more and more nervous and lost over following, with frequent pauses.)* The lecturer's mechanical behaviour is suddenly apparent to us. Yes, and um - this is funny. According to Bergson. Because his – not Bergson's – my – that is, the lecturer's – his, the lecturer's terror – and it is indeed terror – is juxtaposed by the life force. Yes. The thrusting – dynamic indeed – erect – stuff. You know the *stuff* - of *life* - as it were. Ah yes – and the lecturer is left – bereft – bereft of words even – without certainty certainly – for as we know, as Buddhists – words can only point the way – unfortunately – ahhhhh – the lecturer is left – in negative capability as it were – in Keats's – Keats's – Keats's – odd word to keep repeating - repeating – Keats's – apposite phrase – leaving me – him – the lecturer – Keats's – in a bit of a void – which is, of course – em – funny – *(A very long pause, as long as the audience can take and then longer. Doctor Spalding remains staring at the audience, rooted to the spot, his mounting terror evident. He is finally led off.)*

Angulimala: Portrait of a Serial Killer

A short play for the stage

(The set consists of three logs acting as dining room chairs and a long, flat, rough piece of wood acting as a dining table. Various indoor plants to suggest both jungle and suburban gentility. A very serious person enters.)

Very serious person: Good afternoon. And now for some storytelling. This afternoon Sarvananda, Satyadaka and Sam Wilkin are going to tell us the dramatic story of Angulimala. For those of you who don't know the story, Angulimala was a fierce killer who became a disciple of the Buddha and eventually achieved full and perfect enlightenment. The story can be found in the Pali Canon, in the Majjhima Nikaya, book number 12. So, the story of Angulimala will be told based on this Pali Canon source. The story begins thus: "Thus have I heard. At that time, in the depths of the forest, lived the fearsome bandit, Angulimala. He lived near the village of Backkati near the town of Benares and was feared by young and old alike." *(Changing style of delivery)* Ladies and gentlemen, live from the home of British and European boxing, York Hall, would you welcome please, weighing in at 260 pounds, the heavyweight champion of Ancient India, Mister Thumb-necklace himself, Angulimalaaaa!

*(**Angulimala** enters in Hawaiian shirt and leopard skin shorts, grisly thumb necklace around his neck, cleaver in hand, gum shield and, initially, a dressing gown. Salutes audience, postures, shakes a few hands, (perhaps dwelling on the thumbs), etc. Quietens audience down as he removes dressing gown and gum shield.)*

Angulimala: Once in a while, a truly great man is born, a man who changes the course of history. This is the story of one such man. A man very dear to my heart. A man born 2,500 years ago in Ancient India, a man whose name has reverberated down the centuries. That man is *(striking chest)* Angulimala....

(He begins to go into a wild dance, manipulating his cleaver, as he speaks.)

Angulimala: ... terror and scourge of India! Angulimala, of the thumb necklace. Angulimala, the man who all fear and despise yet who all envy for he is in touch with the darkness, the chaos within. As the timid worldlings shiver in their huts, imprisoned by convention and dull habit, it is only Angulimala who dares to act upon his deepest, darkest desires. Only Angulimala has the courage of his spontaneous convictions. Angulimala the terrible! Angulimala the superman! Angulimala who, only one hour ago, slaughtered his ninety ninth victim!

(He yells in triumph, arms outstretched. As he does so, Angulimala's Mum enters, kisses him on the cheek and places a tablecloth over his outstretched arm, thus destroying much of the impact of his dance. Mum is well turned out and has a genteel manner. Wears a little apron or house coat.)

Mum: Morning dear. You're up early.

Angulimala: Aye, well, I had business in the village.

(Together, they put tablecloth over the rough piece of wood)

Mum: I just can't get the stains out of this cloth. I hope you didn't use it to garrot anybody.

(Angulimala sits. Mum puts various bowls, condiments etc. on table. Fusses over table and her son who is constantly fidgeting with energy throughout the play. At the moment he is biting the nails on his necklace.)

Mum: Stop fidgeting dear. You'll upset the things. Sit up properly, Mr. Fidget. And stop biting your nails.

Angulimala: Fuss, fuss, fuss. Any chance of some breakfast? You know, when you have a minute.

(Mum takes a little carton of cereal and deftly pours it into Angulimala's bowl. Adds milk.)

Angulimala: What's this?

Mum: What's it look like?

Angulimala: Looks suspiciously like a very small portion of "Rice Krispies." This is no breakfast for a man, mother. Where's my bacon and eggs? My sausages and bagels?

Mum: Well perhaps, Angulimala dear, if you brought a little money into the hoose we might be able to afford some bagels.

(Angulimala takes a pair of ear-rings from his pocket and dangles them in front of his mother.)

Angulimala: Well, perhaps mother dear, these might go a little way to buying some proper food.

Mum: *(Excited)* Sapphire!

Angulimala: Aye. Sapphire.

Mum: *(She takes them from him.)* Oh, they're very nice son, so they are. Here. Hold on a minute. I recognise those ear-rings. Are these no Deirdre McLuskie's? Have you killed Mrs. McLuskie? Is that where you've been?

Angulimala: Possibly.

Mum: I don't know what to do with you, I really don't. I am speechless. Absolutely speechless. Deirdre McLuskie was my best friend. My bosom pal.

Angulimala: Oh, come on Maw. She wasnae your bosom pal. You was always saying how stuck up she was. Wouldnae give you the time of day when she passed you in the jungle.

Laughing Gravy

Mum: She was the only person left in the village to talk to apart from you, you big hippo. What a senseless waste of human life.

Angulimala: I'll take them back if you don't want them.

Mum: You will not take them back. *(Putting them on).* I want something to remember her by. *(Sighs)* She was so well preserved for her age. All her own teeth. Some really lovely, gold fillings....

(She looks meaningfully at Angulimala who reluctantly removes gold fillings from his pocket and hands them to Mum who places them in her purse.)

Angulimala: Bagels tomorrow, mind. *(Putting ear to cereal).* I thought these were meant to make humorous, wee noises.

Mum: Poor old Deirdre. A woman of innumerable and varied qualities, her passing leaves us all with a profound sense of loss.

(Angulimala chokes on his cereal. Spits free plastic gift into the air.)

Mum: My goodness, what was that? *(She picks it up, looks at it, hands it to Angulimala. Then looks at empty box of "Rice Krispies." Reads.)* "Free with "Rice Krispies." Busts of the great holy men. Set of six. Collect the set." Who have you got?

Angulimala: I'm no that bothered if I'm honest. Bald geezer.

Mum: The Buddha.

Angulimala: The Buddha! *(Spits.)*

Mum: Don't gob on the rug. It marks it.

Angulimala: Busts of the great Indian holy men! They should have busts of the great Indian killers.

Mum: Cereal killers! Get it? *(Laughs. To audience).* I don't make a joke very often but when I do, I hit the nail on the head.

Sarvananda

Angulimala: *(To audience)* I'd like to put a nail through *her* head.

Mum: Pardon?

Angulimala: The Buddha. Well, that's dead ironic right, cos he is going to be my hundredth victim. It's all planned. Then there will be one more victim after him. Victim 101. I wonder who number 101 will be, *mother*? *(Laughs)*.

Mum: What you on about?

Angulimala: And after victim 101, it's time to stop. I'm through with serial killing. Had enough of it. I want a career change.

Mum: And what would you do, dear?

Angulimala: Carpenter. Like Dad was.

Mum: *(Laughs)*

Angulimala: What's so funny?

Mum: Remember that kitchen cabinet you made?

Angulimala: What about it?

Mum: It wasnae flush for a start. Everything slid off the shelves.

Angulimala: My spirit level was broke.

Mum: Spirit level, my eye. The whole thing collapsed after about a week. The thing is son, you're absolutely useless at absolutely everything and you always were. It's not your fault dear. It's the way you were born. *(Tenderly)* As your Daddy used to say, "A coconut for a heid and two bunches of bananas for hands."

Angulimala: Aaaaah! See you? Your days are numbered, hen. *(Pointing to plastic bust)*. He's one hundred. You're 101. You're going to be my last victim. It was going to be a surprise but you push a man beyond the limits of human endurance.

Mum: You're going to kill your mother?

Angulimala: Aye.

Mum: And who'll look after you then?

Angulimala: I'll look after masel.'

Mum: Mm hm? And who's going to give you a cuddle when you're all sad and lonely?

Angulimala: I don't need you.

Mum: "Mammy ! Mammy! Naebody loves me, Mammy! Why can I no get a girlfriend, Mammy?"

(Angulimala puts hands over ears. Mum removes them.)

Mum: You know fine well I'm the only one who loves you. You know fine well you wouldnae last a minute without your Mother. Come on son, give your Mummy a cuddle.

(She puts her arms around him. Angulimala shrugs her off.)

Angulimala: You know why I never got a girlfriend? Because of you. Every lassie I've brought back here, you've abused and insulted.

Mum: You never bring back any nice girls, son. They're all so common.

Angulimala: Carol Murdoch wasnae common. She was beautiful. Soon as we sat doon to dinner, you start telling her about how I wet the bed as a wee boy. Is it any wonder I turned oot as I did?

Mum: Aye, it's always the mother to blame. That's it, son. Blame your mother. Listen, darling. You are the way you are because you're fundamentally hopeless.

Angulimala: *(Roars.) Aaaaaah! (Stands with cleaver. Going into his dance)* Angulimala! Terror and scourge of India! Whose very name makes kings and princes quake in their boots! Just as the mighty lion's roar silences every beast for miles around, so the name of Angulimala strikes every man, woman and child dumb with terror! Angulimala! Hear him call his name! Hear the lion's roar! Angulimala! *(Whispers)* Angulimala…. They whisper his name in fear and trembling…. Hear his name go whispering through the jungle like the breeze… Angulimala…. And like, a serpent, suddenly, he *strikes*! And is gone. *Where* has he gone? Naebody knows. No-one can catch him; he dodges, he ducks, elusive, a shadow, a whisper, his weapon of death dancing in his hand; he dances away, this conjuror of death, this genius of butchery, this killer of the thumb necklace, this Angulimala….

(Slight pause. Then sound of doorbell. Mum looks out window.)

Mum: It's a bhikkhu. Quick, tidy the place up a bit.

*(She goes to door (offstage). Enters with **Bhikkhu**. He wears an orange Hawaiian shirt and shorts. Shades. Carries a begging bowl. Mum is obviously rather taken with him.)*

Bhikkhu: Warm out there.

Mum: Yes, we're having a bit of an Indian summer, aren't we? Roll on the monsoon, eh? Well, it's good for the garden. Excuse the mess. My son and I were having a little breakfast and my son's no the most careful of eaters. Would you care to join us?

Bhikkhu: If it's no trouble.

Mum: No trouble at all. Take a seat. It's always a pleasure. We've had quite a few homeless wanderers pass through.

Angulimala: *(Fingering necklace.)* Numbers 14, 56 and 73 if my memory serves me right.

Bhikkhu: Sorry?

Mum: Excuse my son. *(She taps her head implying madness.)* Now, I'll just go and make some tea, shall I? Sorry, what's your name?

Bhikkhu: I don't really have a name. I've gone forth, you see. From names. From family.

Angulimala: A literal minded bhikkhu. The worst sort.

Mum: Of course. Shame though in a way. Family life can be a constant source of joy. And you'd make some young lady a lovely husband n'that. Still, your decision. Milk and sugar?

Bhikkhu: Black and sweetener. *(Pats stomach.)*

Mum: Very wise. *(Exits)*

Angulimala: No name, eh? So right, you're in the jungle, right, and a monkey chucks a coconut at your baldy heid. And your mate shouts out, "Watch out……" But because you don't have a name, he cannae finish the sentence, and you cop the coconut on the back of your heid. That's just daft, innit?

Bhikkhu: *(Just smiles).*

Angulimala: Well, I've got a name. Want to hear it?

Bhikkhu: *(Nods graciously)*

Angulimala: Angulimala.

(Pause)

Angulimala: Angulimala. Heard of me?

Bhikkhu: Rings a bell.

Angulimala: Okay. Well, you may have noticed this necklace here. About my person.

Bhikkhu: Yes. Unusual.

Angulimala: Yes, it is unusual because these here digits are, in actual fact, the thumbs of my victims. I am Angulimala, the serial killer.

(Mum enters with a tea trolley.)

Mum: Don't point your cleaver at our guest, dear. I'll be mother, shall I?

(Angulimala sulks and sucks thumb. Mum pours the tea with great elegance into the stranger's bowl and rather flirtatiously pops in two sweeteners.)

Bhikkhu: Another one please.

Mum: My goodness. You're very extreme for a bhikkhu. Extremely sweet! *(Removing doyly)* Can I tempt you to a scone?

Angulimala: *Scones?*

Bhikkhu: Thank you.

(Angulimala attempts to take a scone but Mum smacks his hand.)

Bhikkhu: Very nice tea. Very refreshing.

Mum: I'm glad you like it.

Bhikkhu: Your son tells me he's a serial killer.

Mum: Yes, well, he was never very good at anything else you see so he had to fall back on the serial killing. He's a useless big lump, aren't you dear? He doesnae like me saying that, but it's true. You might have seen a heap of wood by the front door. It's a kitchen cabinet he made. *(Laughs)* Oh my goodness. Bananas for hands.

Angulimala: *(Growls)*

Mum: You must excuse my son. We did our best, his daddy and I, but he hasnae quite turned oot how we would have wished.

Angulimala: "Did our best?" Let me tell you something, Mr. Nobody. After I was born, you know what my dear mother and father did? Exposed me in the jungle. Left me to the vultures.

Mum: His daddy, Brahma rest him, was dead set on a wee lassie, you see. Muggins here broke his heart. Being a boy n'that.

Angulimala: Luckily some leopards found me. For two years I was brought up as a leopard cub, as one of their set. So it's no surprising I lack some of the social graces. It's no surprising I drop on all fours in times of crisis and instead of shaking hands at parties, smell people's....

Mum: *(Interrupting.)* Please! I'm sure our guest doesn't want to hear about all your personal hang-ups.

Angulimala: And she has the effrontery to say "we did our best."

Mum: We took you back, didn't we? We took him back to the bosom of the family, you know, Mister... Despite severe financial difficulties.

Angulimala: Only because Dad needed someone to do the chores. By then I was half leopard.

Mum: The ingratitude! What I've sacrificed for that boy. I gave up a promising career as a jazz saxophonist to bring his lordship up. I was part of the famous quintet, the Lumbini Five, you know.

Angulimala: That was a great loss to the Indian sub-continent, wasn't it?

Mum: It's very difficult being a parent. You receive very little thanks from your offspring. I don't suppose you'd know about that, being a homeless wanderer....

Bhikkhu: Actually... *(Passes Mum a photo.)*

Mum: Oh yes. Very nice indeed. My own son never had that sweet look about him. It was always a snarl with him. Now, if you excuse me, I just need to attend to the almond slices. *(Exits.)*

Angulimala: Almond slices? Dear Brahma. She's obviously taken a shine to you, pal. Difficult woman, you know. Difficult woman. Would have ruined my life you know but. Well, I bounce back. I'm very resilient. Anyway, she's no going to be around much longer. Know what I mean? Enjoying that scone, aye?

Bhikkhu: Yes.

Angulimala: "Yes." You don't have much conversation, do you? "Yes. No. Very refreshing." Must be a scintillating life being a bhikkhu. On your full moon nights. When you all get the gither. Real knees up I imagine. "Evening Mr. Nobody." "Oh, evening Mr. Nobody. How are you this evening?" "Fine, and you?" "Fine thanks." *(He looks at bhikkhu, then looks at the plastic bust from the "Rice Krispies" box. Points at bust.)* You're one of his lot, aren't you? Baldy heid and an orange shirt. Well, he's no going to last much longer either. His number's up. Number 100. *(Points offstage towards Mum).* Number 101. Would you stop staring at me, please? Staring and smiling like that. It's very rude. Look, I advise you to leave. Leave now because I'm getting a wee bit irritable and I don't like your face. You don't seem to realise you've stumbled into the hut of Angulimala. I'm constantly in the news, you know. Last week I was on this documentary – "Celebrity Jungle Killers." Don't suppose you saw it? No. I've seen you somewhere before. Where was it? Mmm? *(Getting steadily more agitated. Wields cleaver.)* See this? This is my murder weapon. This is what I do the serial killing with. 99 victims I have despatched with this. You could very well be my century, you know. Was going to make Buddha number one hundred but I'm quite willing to change my plans. In fact, your number's up, pal. That's got you shaking in your sandals, hasn't it, eh? Why don't you speak? Stop staring!... Mum! Where are those almond slices? I know where I've seen you. I had a dream. You were in my dream. Standing in a clearing in the jungle. I came at you with my cleaver. I ran at you. You didnae move. I wanted your thumb. I ran at you with my cleaver to take your thumb and cut your throat. You walked away very slowly. I ran after you. I ran like the wind. But no matter how fast I tried to run, I couldnae catch you. You were just walking. I ran and ran but couldnae catch you. And you turned and smiled. And stopped. And I ran but I couldnae get any closer. And then you looked at me and you said….

Bhikkhu: Stop Angulimala!

(Bhikkhu takes off his shades, takes Angulimala's head in his hands and stares into his eyes. Angulimala is frozen. Then he growls and breaks free.)

Angulimala: Angulimala! Terror and scourge of India! *(Does his dance but slowly winds down as bhikkhu comes towards him.)* Whose very name makes kings and princes quake in their boots! Just as the mighty lion's roar silences every beast for miles around, so the name of Angulimala strikes every man, woman and child dumb with terror… Angulimala… Hear him call his name…. Hear the lion's roar…. Angulimala… Mum?

(Bhikkhu takes Angulimala's head in his hands as before.)

Angulimala: Who are you?

Bhikkhu: You're in hell.

Angulimala: Don't need you to tell me that. *(Backing away from bhikkhu.)* Cannae sleep. Dream of fire. Of being eaten alive by creepy crawlies. Having my teeth pulled oot one by one. Mum's fault. I'm no to blame. Killed a few people, okay. But they'd have died anyway sooner or later. Law of impermanence. You know. What's so great aboot life anyway? Life? Huh! Extremely over-rated in my opinion. Law of the jungle. Kill or be killed…. They come to me at night. Hands outstretched. Thumbs missing. Asking for their thumbs back. Pleading. But what is done cannae be undone. A leopard cannae change his spots!

Bhikkhu: Come with me Angulimala.

Angulimala: *(Has backed into the table. His hand touches the plastic bust.)* You're *him*, aren't you? The man himself. The one who told me to stop. The Buddha.

Bhikkhu: Join my Order.

Angulimala: *(Nervously. Rapidly)* Thought aboot it, you know. No my cup of tea. Anyway, couldnae leave my mother. Don't like the way you and your friends slag off the family. Slag off romantic love. I'm going to retire, find a nice lassie, settle doon, have a family. I'm a great believer in love, me. Love conquers all. And see you. You've no tradition. Made it all up yourself. And I've heard things aboot you and your Order. All left footers if you know what I mean. No chance. And I'm no intae this meditation lark. No intae silence.

Bhikkhu: Why are you so terrified of silence?

Angulimala: Because *I hate myself! (He falls on all fours and howls. Picks himself up.)* Got one of those wee books on improving your self-worth but it didnae help much. I have no qualities at all you see. I did the wee test in the appendix at the back of the book. I scored minus 500 on positive qualities.

Bhikkhu: You're a good mover.

Angulimala: Aye, well I have been known to shake my booty at times, you know…. Got to pull myself together. I am Angulimala!

Bhikkhu: You're going to dance out of here.

Angulimala: Angulimala. I'm Angulimala. Terror and scourge of India.

Bhikkhu: You're going to dance out of here and join us.

Angulimala: And why would I want to do that?

Bhikkhu: Because I'm offering you a way out of hell.

Angulimala: Nah. Nah. You're nothing. Mr. Nobody. I'm no scared of you. Nothing but a number. Number one hundred!

(With a terrible roar, Angulimala grabs cleaver and goes for Bhikkhu who grabs his wrist. Cleaver falls to floor. Music begins. "The Passenger" by Iggy Pop. The struggle develops into a dance, the Bhikkhu mirroring Angulimala's movements. The Bhikkhu is a very good dancer. Angulimala, reluctantly, almost against his will, yet fascinated and hypnotised, begins to mirror Bhikkhu's movements. During the dance, Angulimala takes off his necklace and puts it on table. And they both dance out of the house. Music ends. Pause. Mum comes on with almond slices.)

Mum: Almond slices! *(She looks around)* Hello? Hello? *(She sees the thumb necklace.)* He never takes his necklace off! Not even to sleep! *(Cry of grief)* He's gone! My wee boy! Gone off with that bhikkhu! What'll I do? My wee boy has flew the nest! My heart is broke! What is a mother to do? *(Slight pause.)* Here. *(To audience)* Don't go away. *(Handing member of audience almond slices.)* I've just had a thought. Back in a sec.

(Mum exits and returns with her saxophone. Plays "When the saints go marching in." Angulimala, Bhikkhu and Mum then take their bows. **End of play**.*)*

A short sermon

Minister: Well boys and girls, (and I hope I got that the right way around), it's funny to think, isn't it, that I used to sit where you're sitting now. Yes, as a wee lad, you may not believe this but, as a wee lad, I used to sit in the very pews where you're sitting now and listen to the sermons of my predecessor, the Reverend James Mauchline, no longer with us due to a very unfortunate bobsleigh accident. And I remember one of the Reverend Mauchline's sermons *particularly* well. It was Easter Sunday and the Reverend Mauchline was talking about the crucifixion and resurrection of our Lord. And the image of Jesus which the Reverend Mauchline so vividly painted for us, the picture of Jesus hanging there for our sins, stayed with me. The image of our gentle Lord pinned to that wood made quite an impression on me. Made quite an impression on this young, impressionable mind. And I remember, during lunch that same day, telling my mother and father about the impression the Rev. Mauchline had made on me and I remember saying "Mum, Dad, one day I want to be a Church of Scotland minister. One day I want to stand in that pulpit and tell the story of the crucifixion and resurrection of our Lord."

So here I am. I have realised my dream. Here I am in the pulpit, twenty-five years later, talking to you about the crucifixion and resurrection of our Lord. Although admittedly I haven't started yet. So let me launch into my subject boys and girls without further ado or preamble. Yes, on Easter Friday all those years ago, all those thousands of years ago, (well actually *two* thousand years ago), on that Easter Friday, our Lord was crucified. As we know. Our Lord had to carry his own cross, a blooming heavy thing, a very long way, possibly in bad weather, possibly not. (We don't know the weather at the time. It's not in the scriptures.) Aye, he dragged this very heavy cross to Golgotha, the Place of the Skull, and on that green hill so far away, our dear Lord was crucified. He lay down on the cross and two nails were driven into his wrists. His ankles were broken and his feet tied together and another nail knocked through his feet. Very big nails they must have been, obviously. And the cross was hauled up – probably by means of ropes and pulleys. It's doubtful if scaffolding was used. And Jesus hung there. Bleeding.

I imagine some of you in the hurly burly of life have cut yourself. Cut your hands or your feet perhaps. Perhaps even more painful mishaps have occurred. I know Mr. Robertson, the verger, once had a serious accident with a power saw, an accident from which he still bears very evident and rather frightening scars. And Mr. Robertson will tell you how painful that was. So will Mrs. Robertson. She witnessed it. Well worse, far worse, was our Lord's crucifixion as regards the pain department. Can you imagine being nailed to two pieces of wood and left there to hang and bleed to death? There is a very good film, boys and girls, directed by Hollywood superstar Mel Gibson, called *The Passion of the Christ*. In this film we are shown just how much Jesus suffered. Just how much he bled. It's a film worth watching just for that very reason. Before he was crucified of course, Jesus was scourged, flailed, cut, whipped and punched in the face. Mel Gibson does not flinch from showing us this. This is why it's such a very popular film. It's so true to life. It's the most truly religious film I've ever seen. I think it's also the bloodiest film I've ever seen. Our Lord is literally awash in blood. And we are washed clean in that blood. So, we should be very grateful. Both to our Lord himself and to Hollywood superstar, Mel Gibson.

Anyhow, yes, our Lord was crucified and hung there bleeding and then, to put the icing on the blooming cake, to put the tin lid on it, a nasty man stuck a spear in his ribs. For no apparent reason. Very irresponsible. But then, at this point, another man, a *nice* man, gave our Lord a sponge soaked in vinegar. Not sponge as in cake, but a normal household sponge that you'd use to wash the dishes, and Jesus did suck it and drank from it thereof. The nice man who gave Jesus the sponge soaked in vinegar wasn't being funny. Vinegar was a drink in those days.

Anyway, despite the nice man's generous gesture, Jesus got a bit fed up, and who can blame him, and he said, *"My God, my God, why hast thou forsaken me?"* He was probably very hungry too. He hadn't had any lunch. And not long after that, maybe about five o'clock, just about tea time, our Lord said, *"Father forgive them for they know not what they do."* And then he said *"It is over."* And then, yes, he died. Without even having had his tea. He died quite quickly due probably to all the blood he had lost.

Now so far, I have just described the crucifixion. But of course, there is also the resurrection. I remember very well what the Reverend James Mauchline said about the resurrection. He said it was a nice fairy story. And, like my predecessor, I'm not going to beat about the bush boys and girls. You are, after all, adults. The resurrection is just that. A nice fairy story to read at bed time – and that has its place, of course. But the message we take from our Lord's story is that life is unrelieved suffering. It is one great big crucifixion as it were, a massive haemorrhage, and only through being washed in the blood of the Lord can we hope to be saved.

Family Values
A short play for the stage

(Suburban living room. A small dining table set for supper - and two chairs. A little table on which is a phone and a phone book. Mum enters with two plates of food. She puts them on the dining table proudly, then takes a tape measure from her apron and measures the distance between each of the chairs and the table. She adjusts the chairs so that they are three feet from the table. Takes off apron.)

Mum: Dinner's ready!

(Dad enters)

Dad: Something smells nice.

Mum: Probably the food, dear. Well, see you later. I'm off to my crazy-paving class.

Dad: In the car I suppose? As usual?

Mum: In the car. Where is the car?

Dad: In the garage, dear. As usual.

Mum: That's a relief.

Dad: Have fun.

(They kiss each other on the cheek from a distance of approximately three yards.)

Dad: Don't do anything I wouldn't do.

(Mum leaves. Dad sits down and begins to eat, although he doesn't move his chair nearer the table. The journey from mouth to plate is thus a bit risky. Enter Bob. He sits at table and engages similarly with the food.)

Bob: Hi.

Dad: Hi.

Bob: Excuse me, but I'm sure I've seen your face somewhere before. What's your name?

Dad: Dad.

Bob: Ah yes! Dad. Dad. How's it going Dad?

Dad: Fine. Fine.

Bob: Good. Good.

(Pause)

Bob: Good.

Dad: You're Bob.

Bob: Yes Dad. I'm Bob.

Dad: I never forget a face, Bob. I forget numbers and keys. Never faces.

(Pause)

Bob: Been up to much, Dad?

Dad: Well yesterday I watched a very good programme on the television, Bob. It was about a bank robbery. The villains got away with half a million pounds in soft furnishings.

Bob: Oh, I think I've seen that. That was yesterday?

Dad: Yes.

Bob: I did see that. In here.

Dad: That's right.

Bob: We watched it together.

Dad: Yes.

Bob: You fell asleep during the panel discussion afterwards.

Dad: Ah yes. Yes.

(Pause)

Dad: Interesting?

Bob: What?

Dad: The panel discussion afterwards?

Bob: Not really. I couldn't make out what the Dalai Lama was saying. And the Queen Mother got a bit irascible.

(Pause)

Bob: I've been wondering Dad.

Dad: Yes Bob?

Bob: Ehm. I mean shoot me down in flames, and I wouldn't bring the subject up if Mum was here, but I wonder if it wouldn't be more comfortable if we pulled the chairs nearer the table.

Dad: *(Laughs)* You young ones, eh?

Bob: I was just thinking we might get more food in our mouths.

Dad: We've always eaten this way, son.

Bob: Yes, I know but....

Dad: What do you think your mother would say if her crazy paving class was cancelled and she came home early and found the two of us sitting nearer the table? Eh?

Bob: I know but...

Dad: Come on son. Don't be so selfish.

Bob: It's all right when it's a kind of dry, solid meal. But when there's a sauce or gravy, it's just....

Dad: Son. That's enough. Where do you think I got my sense of balance from?

Bob: Yes. Sorry.

Dad: I remember having exactly the same conversation with *my* father. That man's sense of balance was unbelievable. I never saw him drop so much as a sprout. Not even in his old age when his faculties were not all they could have been.

(Phone rings)

Dad: What's that?

Bob: The phone.

Dad: *(Getting up)* No, I mean *who's* that? Phoning in the middle of our supper?

Bob: I hope it's no-one famous.

Dad: *(Answering phone)* 754398?

(Bob waves at Dad)

Dad: Hang on a minute. My son is making frantic, waving motions in my direction. *(To Bob)* What is it?

Bob: We're not 754398.

Dad: Aren't we?

Bob: No.

Dad: What are we?

Bob: 672966.

Dad: Really?

Bob: Yes.

Dad: *(Into phone)* Hello? Sorry, seemingly we're 672966, not 754398.

(Pause)

Dad: *(To Bob)* She says "Who's 754398 then?"

Bob: Tell her I'll look it up in the phone book.

(Bob gets up and looks in the phone book.)

Dad: My son will look it up in the phone book for you. It might take some time.

(Pause. Bob searches phone book.)

Bob: Who is it?

Dad: Who is it what?

Bob: Who is it on the other end of the line?

Laughing Gravy

Dad: *(Into phone)* Could I ask who's calling please? *(To Bob)* It's your mother.

Bob: Ah. Here we are. 754398. J. Mulholland. 23 Riddrie Crescent. Riddrie.

Dad: *(Into phone)* Hello dear. You want a Mr. J. Mulholland. 23 Riddrie Crescent. Riddrie. Yes. 754398. Yes. Bye then dear. Bye.

(Dad puts phone down)

Dad: There's something wrong somewhere.

Bob: No Dad. It says it here. 754398. J. Mulholland. 23 Riddrie Crescent. Riddrie.

(They sit back down at table. Phone rings.)

Dad: *(Getting up)* Goodness me, we're popular tonight. *(Picks up phone)* 627966?

(Bob gives Dad thumbs up for getting number correct)

Dad: Oh, hello dear. Yes, I couldn't *quite* understand…. Yes, I'll ask Bob. Sometimes a university degree makes all the difference. *(Laughs. To Bob)* What was it your mother was phoning Mr. Mulholland about?

Bob: I don't know. She'll have to ask him.

Dad: Bob doesn't know dear. He suggests you ask Mr. Mulholland. Yes. Yes. Bye then. *(Puts phone down.)* Your mother seems a bit confused.

Bob: Isn't she at her crazy paving class?

Dad: Evidently not.

(The doorbell rings)

Dad: Good grief.

Bob: I'll get it Dad. You've already got it twice.

Dad: But your dinner's getting cold, son.

Bob: So's yours, Dad.

Dad: But I've eaten more than you. And you had all that stress with the phone book. I think, taking everything into account, I should get it, Bob. This time. I know you'd do the same for me.

Bob: Okay, Dad. Thanks.

(Dad picks up phone)

Dad: 672966? Hello? Hello? *(Puts phone down.)* Line's gone dead.

Bob: That's the phone you picked up Dad.

Dad: *(Confused)* Yes....

(Doorbell rings again)

Dad: Flipping heck! It's like Liverpool Street Station at the rush hour!

(Bob exits to answer door. Phone rings.)

Dad: Flipping heck!

(Dad answers phone.)

Dad: 754398?... No, I'm not Mr. Mulholland dear. I think you're a bit confused.

(Dad puts phone down. Sits at table. Enter Bob and the prophet. The prophet wears a white robe and has a long, grey beard.)

Bob: This is Mr. Zukerman Dad, and he's come to tell us something.

Dad: *(Irritably)* Tell us something or sell us something?

Bob: Pertinent point.

Prophet: *(Proclaiming)* There's a great spiritual vacuum all over the land!

Bob: We've already got one thank you.

Dad: What did I tell you?

(Phone rings. Prophet picks it up.)

Laughing Gravy

Prophet: Hello?... Yes. Yes. Yes, well Browning's verse doesn't stay in the mind like that of other poets, it's true. But he had a very honed sense for the dramatic... Yes. Indeed.... Hang on.

(Prophet motions for a pad and pencil which Bob supplies. Prophet writes.)

Prophet: Yes. Yes.... That's all clear.... Yes.... *(Puts phone down. To Dad.)* That was your wife. *(Reading off pad)* She says can you pick her up because the car broke down outside B and Q on the way to the crazy paving class? Mr. Mulholland...

Dad: 23 Riddrie Crescent.

Prophet: Mr. Mulholland can't give her a lift because A) he's giving a dinner party and B) he doesn't know your wife from Adam. Or Eve presumably.

Dad: That settles that then.

Bob: What settles what?

Dad: Not really sure.

(Bob and Dad look to prophet for guidance. Slight pause)

Prophet: All shall be swept away! The deadening rituals of family life will soon be things of the past... Eh....

(Pause. Prophet has lost his confidence a bit.)

Prophet: The new order's upon us!

Bob: Did you come here by car Mr. Zuckerman?

Prophet: Yes.

Bob: Can we borrow it?

Prophet: Eh....

Bob: *(To Dad)* I don't know how Mum expected us to pick her up if we've only got one car.

Dad: In a taxi perhaps.

Bob: Is your car a taxi?

Prophet: It is, actually.

Dad: That's a bit of luck.

(Prophet gives Dad the keys.)

Prophet: It sticks in third.

Dad: We won't be long. Pray to heaven we're not too late.

Bob: Too late for what?

Dad: Eh…

(They look to prophet for guidance. Pause.)

Prophet: *(Hesitantly)* Well… As long as you are breathing, it is never too late to start, you know… living…. *(Beat)* Possibly.

Bob: We better get a move on then Dad.

(Dad and Bob rush out. Embarrassed pause as prophet looks at audience. Eventually he sits on one of the chairs. Looks round to see if anyone is looking.)

Prophet: Well, as Friedrich Nietzsche once said….

(He pulls chair close to table.)

Prophet: "Live dangerously."

(He begins to eat)

(Black out. End of play)

Superhero

Compere (Satyadaka): Bhante, our teacher, has always emphasized the importance of extending the hand of fellowship to other groups and this afternoon we are delighted to welcome someone from an organisation which was also founded in 1967. The organisation is *The Supra Personal League of Super Heroes* and our guest this afternoon is…Blazing Comet.

(Blazing Comet enters in rather tight-fitting costume. Does a Blazing Comet dance and puts his back out. Beckons to compere who puts his knee in small of Blazing Comet's back and pushes.)

Blazing comet: Good afternoon. It's a privilege and pleasure to be invited to your gathering on the occasion of your fiftieth anniversary. My own movement, the Supra Personal League of Super Heroes, sometimes rather facetiously referred to by its acronym *SPLOSH,* was also founded in 1967. What we often do in our own movement is give a little talk on why we are a Super Hero or why we became involved in *SPLOSH* - so I'd like to do that for you now.

So, before I became Blazing Comet, my old name was Clark Trent and I was working as a trainee journalist for the *London Daily Planet*. I had just left school and this was 1967. And I was quite troubled. Because I had certain gifts that I couldn't talk to anyone about. I had begun to notice, for example, that I knew what people were going to say before they said it. I also became very aware, early on, of a troublesome tendency to radiate heat when I was angry. Or aroused. And this had led to scalding problems with my boss - and also my first, and only, girlfriend. As well as all this, I found I had a certain degree of X-Ray vision which, being a young man with troublesome hormones, I didn't always use appropriately. I could see through clothing and this got me aroused which led to overheating problems which led to yes, some people being scalded. The upshot of all this was I thought I was going crazy, I started drinking, and I really did start to go downhill.

But luckily, I just happened to see a little advert in the newspaper I was working for. I think it just said something like: *Harness your super powers. Free class. Tea and biscuits* and it gave an address in Monmouth Street in London. So, I went along and it was all very low-key. The class took place in a little basement flat and was led by this bloke who looked a bit hippyish and who introduced himself as Captain Wonder. Or just, The Captain. So, over the next few weeks The Captain introduced me, and several others, to various simple exercises. Including the mindfulness of sense powers where we'd learn to taste colours, see sounds and touch our thoughts. There were also the communication exercises where we'd sit opposite one another and communicate using nonsense phrases. And then move on to using nonsense smells. And another exercise where we'd transfer our consciousness into an inanimate object, like a block of cheese, say. You know, we'd all have a block of cheese - like Gorgonzola or Feta - and we'd attempt to transfer our awareness into the cheese and animate it. And this exercise was called the Feta Bhavana.

I think what impressed me most about those early days was Captain Wonder's small acts of kindness. He gave us his time. He really listened. After one of those first evenings, I remember going up to him and saying that I had all these things going on, and I felt I was going mad. I had X-Ray vision and I could read people's minds and what was I going to do with all these crazy powers? And he smiled kindly and simply said, "Use your powers for the benefit of mankind." And I said, "I knew you were going to say that," and he laughed, and it kind of broke the ice.

But I think what finally persuaded me to ask to become a committed Super Hero was a seminal lecture Captain

Wonder gave called *Nietzsche, Man and Superman.* Incredibly inspiring, and actually, I think quite a few of us committed ourselves after hearing that talk. David Johnson, who became The Black Lynx, was there. So was ex-Debbie Mackenna from Edinburgh, who became Rubber Woman. Alex Boothroyd, who became Mister Invisible. (Haven't seen him for ages actually). And of course, myself - Blazing Comet. So, I was given a new name - and the appropriate costume. And this is what Captain Wonder said when he gave me my name:

"The ex-Clark Trent is a very mild-mannered man. Indeed, he is so still and quiet that on more than one occasion some of us have assumed that he has had a stroke or even passed on, as it were. But still waters run deep and underneath that still exterior, the ex-Clark has a lot of energy, indeed one might say that he has a fiery energy, indeed a blazing energy. So, the ex-Clark becomes Blazing Comet. A torch to light the way in these dark times."

I was quite naïve in those early days. I thought my life as a Super Hero would be… well, not *easy* necessarily, but clear-cut. You know, I would fight crime, evil and darkness wherever I found it. But immediately I joined SPLOSH there were some quite practical problems. Like where to keep my keys and loose change. The tightness of my costume also meant that coughing was sometimes a problem and certain old habits - like sexual craving and the subsequent overheating and so on, those habits just carried on, again aggravated by the tightness of my suit. Not to put too fine a point on it. Also, I found members of the general public projected on to me and assumed that I was perfect. I'm not perfect. And some people were - scalded.

And we had various crises in the movement. Mike Hardcastle, who became the Human Volcano, was seduced to the dark side, changed his name to Doctor Doom and sought world domination. And sent many of us toxic mind-rays. As well as some pretty upsetting e-mails. Of course, the forces of good prevailed and Doctor Doom and his evil cohorts were finally subjugated, the Doctor himself meeting a very unpleasant end at the hands of Shrinking Woman, being reduced finally to the size of a small garden pea.

I think one thing I've learnt after all these years is that the nature of good and evil isn't so clear cut. Often one's own superpowers are also one's failings. And I have done some things of which I am very ashamed. And I know we have also had to come to terms with Captain Wonder's shadow side.

I'm getting older of course. The super powers are dimming a bit. I'm getting forgetful. I've started to put my underpants on over my trousers, for example. But I have never regretted getting involved. Meeting so many interesting people who became good friends. I've never regretted meeting Captain Wonder, those fifty years ago. And I am so grateful for his kindness and for handing back to a scared and crazy boy - his life.

Death: a case for the defence
A monologue for radio

Snatches of music, voices, white noise, crackling as we explore various wavebands. We alight on "Blue Skies" – Ella Fitzgerald version. Titles over this. More white noise. until we settle on Death.

DEATH: Hello? Hello? Ah…. At last. Sorry to interrupt whatever you were listening to. I won't be long. Half an hour. At the very most. Yes. Um, look, I know you've got it tough at the moment and I'm probably the last person you want to listen to right now. In fact, you're probably thinking I have a real nerve to show my face at all but eh… No hang on, I haven't actually said who I am, have I? Sorry. No. So. First things first. My name is Death. And as for showing my face... Well, we're on radio – obviously - so just to fill in the picture a bit… I'm not particularly scary-looking. Not gaunt or cadaverous or anything. Not a skeleton with a big black cloak and a scythe and an hour-glass and all that. No. If you saw me in the street, you'd probably not give me a second glance. Well, actually, you might. You might throw me a coin from a distance or something. Because I'm kind of – down and out. Bit shabby the truth be told. I haven't replenished my wardrobe for quite a while. Millennia. Trousers held together by rope, holes in the boots, battered bowler hat. You get the picture. Stained cardigan. Tattered suit.

Partly, it's a self-esteem issue, my appearance. Poor self-view. If you're as unpopular as I am, if people are constantly throwing mud at you, some of it's bound to stick. And as much as I'd *like* to disregard the opinions of others – you know – I'm only human. Actually, that's not true. I'm not human, am I? I don't know how I'd describe myself. Archetypal doesn't quite do it. But like any *human* being, more particularly any human being who's unfortunate enough to have an unpopular job; like *them* and like *you* and like *anyone*, I do have a desire to be *loved.* And I don't think that's unreasonable even if I am, strictly speaking, archetypal. Or whatever the word is.

So, the reason I'm here tonight is to appeal to your generosity. I know, I know. Not another appeal. But I'm not appealing for money. I'm not even appealing for your time. I'm merely appealing for *(Beat)* love. I say this with a certain embarrassment. I know it sounds a little *needy* but the fact is, I'm at the end of my tether. As I hope I shall make clear.

When I say that I'm unpopular, this of course is a massive understatement. The merest hint of my presence seems to put people into a blind panic. Even to mention my name – seemingly – brings bad luck. Fact is, I am universally hated. And that's difficult, you understand? It is not a pleasant thing to be universally despised. So. Fairly recently, just after Covid kicked off, as part of a long overdue PR exercise, to raise my profile and make friends, I created a *Facebook* page. To date, it has had 2 billion, 346 million, 754 thousand 305 dislikes. And two likes. One of those likes was from a very disturbed masochist from Munich and the other was from a hermit who lives in a cave in Sumatra. God knows what he was doing on *Facebook*. God knows how he got a Wi Fi connection. The abuse I've had on that *Facebook* page. Absolutely vitriolic. When I am just doing my job. And recently it's just got worse and worse.

So, I thought I'd turn up in person. Appeal to you personally. Rather than attempt to negotiate the minefield of social media. Make a personal connection. Tell you a bit about my life as a way of helping you *sympathise.* And confess something. Something I'm not proud of. *(Sighs)* I mean, you seem sympathetic. You're still listening. You haven't switched off. And if you want to make a sandwich or a cup of tea while I'm talking, you know, feel free. I've got a tube of *Pringles* here myself. I want you to feel relaxed around me. You know, I'm really not that scary.... *(Crunches a crisp.)*

Yes. So. Here we go. I know you should never really have to justify your own existence. But that's what I'm going to attempt to do today. And in justifying my own existence, I'm going to inevitably have to offer a critique of someone else's existence. That is my twin brother – God. The Creator. Born five minutes before me. And what a difference five minutes can make. I tell you.

God is more popular than me. Another massive understatement. For one thing, he has, it must be said, *charisma*. And he always looks the bees' knees. Always wears white gloves, a white fedora thing, soft as snow, and a resplendent white suit. You will never see a micro deposit of fluff on that white suit – let alone soup, gravy or heaven forbid, saliva. White suit, manicured nails, beautifully barbered beard, and moustache. White, shiny teeth. When he smiles, which is often, it's like a glorious, bright dawn. You feel concussed. Dazzling, sunny, winning smile.

Anyway. Immediately he's born, he just starts creating stuff. I've hardly stuck my head out the womb door after him before I find him *fashioning* loads and loads of *stuff* and, you know, *objects* and dividing stuff from other stuff. The Heaven from the Earth and the day from the night and the light from the dark. *"Let there be a firmament in the midst of the waves"* and so there's a firmament in the midst of the waves. *"And let there be lights in the midst of the firmament"* and lo, lights doth appear in the midst of the firmament. Very quickly he becomes intoxicated. *"Let there be mountains. Hills. Big rocks. Wee rocks let there be. Deserts. Forests. Lakes. Swamps. Rivers. Ponds. Snowdrops. Weeds. Hedges – and shrubbery and foliage in general."* And after this first burst, God seeth what he hath created and saith, *"Lo, it is good."* Though to me it all seems pretty random and indiscriminate, you know? Anyway, he just keeps going.

Och! Foodstuffs. Winged fowl. Creeping things. Beasts of the earth. It's all going to his head and when it does come into his head, he just makes it appear. Koala bears. Ostriches. Kangaroos. Honestly, kangaroos! Cheetahs. Rabbits. And not content with what he's created he says to what he's created *"go forth be fruitful and multiply."* So, they go forth and they are fruitful and they multiply. And multiply. Especially the rabbits.

And then, to put the tin lid on it, he creates Man to have dominion over them all. And *in his own image*, which is the height of arrogance if you ask me. And after he creates Man, he creates Woman out of Man's rib and says to them both *"Go forth, be fruitful and multiply"* and well… They're as bad as the rabbits. And there's God, like a bearded Santa Clause, distributing his bounty and everybody grateful and thankful. *"Keep it coming God, we promise to behave and multiply. If you just keep it coming."* And so, he just keeps it coming. And coming. *"Have a pomegranate. Have a strawberry."* Multiply. Multiply. You get the picture.

But. At some point *I* come into the picture. I start *subtracting.* Like God, no big plan. Just intuitively start removing stuff. As *he*'d started creating stuff. I started quite early on with Abel, (Adam and Eve's eldest.) I had Cain wallop him over the head with a house brick. I knew it wouldn't go down well with God but actually he didn't say anything. I think even he realised that I might just possibly be necessary. To balance out his over-abundance and pathological need for love. Even he realised where there is creation, there must be destruction. Otherwise, we have a problem. So, he kept quiet. He put up with me. He realised *I'd* get the stick; *I'd* be unpopular while he'd still be adored. So, no real problem at first. I found I had a talent for subtraction, just as my brother had a talent for creation. You know. I like space. I don't like clutter. But – I just couldn't keep up with him. I tried to be temperate but he just… Create, create, create, behold, behold, behold…. He was producing stuff far faster than I could harvest it. Until I finally cracked. This was when the tension really started. With the dinosaurs.

Basically, I harvested the lot. As I say, I work intuitively. There was no great plan here. I just found myself sending a massive asteroid hurtling straight at the earth. It landed in Mexico – near what is now the small village of Chicxulub, *(Cheek-sha-lube)*, a popular home for the retired now, seemingly. Anyway, WHAM, the equivalent of 100 trillion tons of TNT or 1 billion Hiroshimas. Tyrannosaurus Rex, Pterodactyl, Brontosaurus, Triceratops. Finished. One Tuesday afternoon this was. And then I get a message from God asking me to come up and have a word - over a working lunch. So, I go up to Heaven, up to his office, very nice big office, acres of spotless carpet, a huge squeaky couch, with a tank of tropical fish and lots of shiny indoor plants – and I can see that God is sore wrath. But he's trying to hide it with his compassionate smile. And, after a light salad, he comes to the point. *"Why did you harvest the dinosaurs?"* And I start to feel sore wrath myself and I just let rip: *"Well for God's sake, God,"* I say. *"What were you thinking creating them in the first place? Take your Brontosaurus. Enormous, fat, clumsy, stupid thing, the brain the size of a pea, blundering into trees, falling over its own feet, squashing everything flat. Dinosaurs? Absolute joke. A blundering pointless screw-up. An evolutionary dead end. Time for them to go."* I really let him have it. And he just smiles and nods. To be honest, I think he can be a bit scared of me. And he says *"Thank you for your time."* And we shake hands and that was that. *"Let's keep in touch,"* he says. But it was never really the same with him after that. Occasional e-mail, phone call. And then we really fell out. When I took a holiday…. This is the confession bit. *(Sighs)* Oh dear. I'll come back to that.

Bottom line. God does not like any of his creation to disintegrate. He hangs on to everything. Talk about anally retentive. If he had his way, he wouldn't let anything go. He is constipated. Literally. Fact you never hear about God. He spends three hours a day on the throne and we are not talking about the celestial seat here; we're talking about something far more down to earth. He wants to hold on to *everything* you see. If one of his creation dies, if I harvest anyone, it's all *boo hoo, boo hoo.* Tragedy. She was struck down at the tender age of 93. Black arm-bands. Bowed heads. *Sniffle, sniffle. Boo hoo.* Tragedy is God's domain. Not mine. *(Gently. Kindly)* I mean, and I know I'm biased, there's a sense of appropriateness when someone dies. There can be a relief there often. That's not cruel. I'm not cruel. Yes, yes, the miracle of birth but let's hear it for the appropriateness of death. And decay. And dissolution. And endings, especially when things have gone on too long. *(Crunches a crisp.)*

Look, in the olden days I was still hated but at least some of the Ancients could see I provided *balance*. All this Covid stuff. I mean, if God and his favourite creatures, (because God made his favourite creatures in his own image), insist on wanting and creating more and more *stuff*, it's going to cause problems. So. For example. With overpopulation and animal habitats ransacked and industrial farming and all the rest of it, animal viruses that are usually contained are going to spill over into humans. Thus, Covid. Actions have consequences. But why should I get blamed for it all when I'm just trying to do my job? Trying to balance things out. Raise a red flag or two.

I don't want to preach to you or lay a guilt trip on you. I know this is difficult to hear but look, I'll let you into a secret. Everything is impermanent. Nothing lasts. Everything decays and dies. God and his favourite creatures, (and pardon me but that includes yourself), cannot face this. But the fact that nothing lasts is what makes something beautiful. I reckon. Its transience. If I can wax a bit lyrical. Don't you think?

But with God…. There is no love of decay. Everything has to be new and shiny. Everything has to be replaced when it starts ageing. While paradoxically, he can never quite let anything go. So, it all gets filed away. For a rainy day. Or stuck in a cupboard. Or booted down to Hades. You know. Where I live. I'm constantly dodging falling microwaves. Hardly anything wrong with them. I put up *"No fly tipping"* signs but he just ignores them. So, more stuff. And more stuff. And more stuff. And I am simply exhausted at trying to temper my brother's excesses. So recently, this was about a hundred years ago, I took a holiday.

Bit of a parable this. Bit of a cautionary tale. I'm very embarrassed about it all. Never told anyone this before. Summer of 1913. It wasn't planned. It started with a bad mistake. I was just so tired. It happened initially cos I got my dates mixed up. I arrived for this bloke a day early. Nice guy called Eric Braithwaite – carpenter - and an artist in his spare time. I turn up at his house expecting him to be at Death's Door and he's all hale and hearty and I say to him, *"Hello Mr. Braithwaite. I'm Death. Are you ready to go?"* and he says he's feeling fine and I realise I've got the wrong day. And I apologise profusely to him and his wife who are both understandably a bit shaken up and I ask them if I can do anything to make it up to them. And Eric's wife, Margaret says *"Do you have to take him at all?"* And I say it would be against all the protocol. Not to take him. But we get talking and they give me some scones and jam and cream and before I know it, I'm pouring my heart out. Saying how I'm so unpopular and misunderstood and so on. And Margaret says*, "Look we've got a spare bed – you're obviously exhausted, why not have a little holiday, give Eric another fortnight, it's not long, you and he can enjoy a game of golf, and you can play with Dennis"* – (who's their little kiddy, nice little kiddy, who I'd taken a bit of a shine to) - and the upshot was I had a holiday. It all went very well at first. I just relaxed. Played hide and seek with wee Dennis. I spent three hours in a cupboard at one point because he'd forgotten all about me. *(Laughs.)* Not very dignified you might say, Death crouching in a cupboard all morning, but I didn't mind. Played golf with Eric. He did a couple of portraits of me too. And I spent time just chatting to Margaret. *(Beat)* And then, well…. A fortnight turned into a month. A month turned into two. Fact is. I'd fallen in love. It was the first time anyone had been really nice to me you see. She wasn't the least bit scared of me either. Her affection, her understanding, her cooking... We started to take long walks. Hold hands. One thing led to another. Until the day Eric came home early from a carpentry job. And there we were, Margaret and I, in the marital bed. *(Beat)* Eric was upset. Understandably, you know. He said, *"To be cuckolded in my own home. Not even by a mortal but the Grim Reaper himself."* He felt utterly betrayed. And the next day he took a shotgun, went into a neighbouring field, put the barrel against his head and fired. *(Beat)* And missed. He fired the other barrel and missed again. In the next few days, he attempted to hang himself, poison himself, stab himself, throw himself from the top of a cliff, set fire to himself, club himself to death with a shovel, throw himself in front of a horse, suffocate himself and, when each of these attempts somehow came to nothing, drown himself. He took the train to the Clyde coast, hired a rowing boat, and threw himself into the sea. Immediately a porpoise took Eric on his back and, despite Eric's valiant efforts, carried him safely to shore.

You see, it was only then that Eric understood. I was on holiday. Death was on holiday. And Eric's inability to die, to kill himself wasn't an isolated incident. All over the world would be suicides were frustrated at every turn. And not just that. People with incurable diseases suddenly recovered. Exhausted old men and old women, struggling for breath on their death beds, lingered on a little longer, and then a little longer, and then a little longer still... All over the globe, wars were taking a very strange turn. Guns and cannons were jamming, bullets were failing to find their mark.... A window cleaner in New York fell from the thirtieth floor of a skyscraper and landed on a bale of hay. The infant mortality rate plummeted to nothing. Violent criminals and murderers cheated the hangman's noose. Etcetera. Population creeping up and up and up.

Laughing Gravy

But my holiday continued. Couldn't tear myself away. I was deeply in love. I'd broken my own cardinal rule never to have favourites. I remember blurting out to Margaret over dinner one evening. *"I will love you forever."*

Eventually God sent the Archangel Michael down to have a word. Nice guy the archangel, if a bit flash. And Michael said *"Your brother's freaking out up there, mate."* And I said – bit sarcastic cos I felt a bit guilty to be honest – "Oh I'm necessary now, am I?" And Michael says, *"In a word, Yes. Things are getting out of hand, Death."* But I couldn't break with Margaret. Well, it all came to a head one morning. I was just sitting in the kitchen with Margaret. We were holding one another's hands and gazing sadly into one another's eyes. And Eric comes in with a drawing. A drawing of me and Margaret. And in the drawing, I'm sitting there holding hands with her. But Margaret had aged in Eric's drawing. He'd drawn her not just old, but ancient. Perhaps one hundred and eighty, bent and bowed, her wrinkled skin hanging from her face in folds. Desperation in her eyes. And coming out of my mouth a caption – *"I'll love you forever."* And that finally snapped me out of it. What was I doing? *(Sighs)* So I just says to Eric, very formally, *"All right Mr. Braithwaite, time for your coronary."* And despite Margaret's protestations I took Eric by the hand and walked out. Didn't look back. And that was that. Felt a bit bitter after that. Kind of lost it. What with the First World War and the Spanish Flu. Second World War not long after.

And God and I just cut off communication completely after that debacle. But I learned my lesson. All very unprofessional, very embarrassing. (Glad to get it off my chest, actually.) And you think God would have learned his lesson too. But no. Just creating more and more and more stuff. And his creatures doing the same. Till these days. Personal computers, personal this, personal that, everyone gets a phone. Two cars. Forests plundered. Oceans cluttered. You know the story. So, what's a guy to do, you know? In the past forty years alone I've been forced to harvest half the planet's wildlife. And now Covid and…. Och, things are not bonny. We've got the balance wrong and it's not *my* fault.

Fact is, God isn't very bright when it comes down to it. Yes, he knows a lot. He's omniscient. He's the sort of guy you'd want on your side on a pub quiz. Who won the FA Cup in 1954? God would have the answer at his fingertips. Name the entire inhabitants of the Glasgow suburb of Netherlee. God could reel them off in alphabetical order. But as for wisdom… That's a different kettle of fish. To be *wise* you have to know a bit about dissolving and grief and sadness and letting go.

Look, I'm almost done. I don't want to take up much more of your time but I do want to say a few things *about* wisdom. And here we're going to get a bit philosophical. I've been writing this book for over five hundred years now. My *magnum opus* – *"Death: a case for the defense."* I have some of it here.

(Sound of paper rustling)

Still in manuscript form. Well, when I say manuscript, it's been written over the centuries on scraps of paper and napkins. Often covered in jam I'm afraid. I tend to be most inspired around breakfast time. But in chapter two here…. Can't quite make it out… But in chapter two I make an important distinction between the realm of Stuff and the realm of the Stuffless. The realm of Stuff is God's realm. Whether it be fridges, zebras, opinions, thoughts, grapes…. Whereas I'm interested in the dissolving of Stuff into the Stuffless.

Put it another way. God is interested in clouds. I'm interested in the blue sky. This is the central metaphor in my work. Clouds and sky. Now, it wouldn't be so bad if God took all these clouds a little less seriously. But there he is up in Heaven fashioning clouds. And getting all attached to them. And his favorite creatures doing the same and giving them names. This is a duck. This is Communism. Fascism. Mars

Bar. And taking these insubstantial clouds very seriously indeed. Duck. Communism. Mars Bar. When it's all just *play* you see. Just making stuff out of cotton wool. Out of thin air. But with God and his favorite creatures, it all gets so heavy that you can't see the sky for the clouds. So, I'm constantly Mr. Spoilsport dissolving it all. Saying, *"Let it go, let it go. "*

And the main problem, the deep stupidity inherent in all this pertains to a *particular* cloud. The *ME* cloud. This is me. My. Mine. And this little me cloud then becomes terrified of its own dissolution. It thinks – or *you* think because the cloud is a metaphor for God and his creatures including *you* – you think you're primarily a tiny cloud. Terrified of dissolving. Whereas in fact you are primarily sky. First and foremost. So, when the cloud dissolves, it's still part of the sky. The sky's still there. And when you *realise* that, then you can start playing, taking it all a little bit more lightly. Now I'm this. Now I'm that. Come together and dissolve. Stuff and Stuffless. Cloud and sky. You can start creating really interesting shapes. It all gets quite beautiful, you know, playful. When you get into the swing of forming and dissolving and letting it all happen. Kissing the joy as it flies, as the poet once said. Kissing the clouds as they fly. And letting all this go too. I mean all these metaphors, cloud, and sky, allow them to die when they've had their time. Because there's nothing worse than a metaphor that overstays its welcome, I always say.

So. I'm about to take my leave now. But. What I've been trying to get at this afternoon is basically – a plea to embrace me. Okay, I'm in a bit of a state. My socks need changing. The suit's falling apart and the beard's horrible. I might not be immediately apparent as a – catch. But let me in. Be my friend. I need a few friends. Let stuff dissolve and die and enjoy the dissolving. You know. Is all I'm saying. And when you make friends with me, get to know me, you might be surprised. I might start appearing a little more attractive. I can introduce you to the Stuffless. It's a realm you can't quite imagine you're so embroiled with stuff. You can't imagine a life without stuff. You assume the Stuffless is nothing at all, just a deadness. Whereas it's the opposite. The Stuffless is alive. And if you fully embrace me…. Then I can retire. And I desperately want to retire. You've found a cure for death. No more death. No God either. What a relief. Just the eternal moment, whatever that is. If you take a deep breath and just put up with the body odour and the smell of mildew, I can be a gateway to the truly wonderful and mysterious. All I'm saying.

Thank you so much for your time. I'll let you continue with your listening. Bye now, take care and see you – well see you *some* time. Later rather than sooner, eh?

Death *crunches a crisp. Brief sound of various wavebands. We alight on "Mister Blue Sky" by Electric Light Orchestra. Then titles over this. A little white noise.*

<u>End of play</u>

Concluding remarks

The Reverend Thompson *is a Church of Scotland minister. He is very earnest and very eager to please.*

THE REV.THOMPSON: So, without further ado, it's my privilege and indeed my pleasure tonight, as chairman of this Ecumenical and Multi Faith Peace Symposium, to bring the events to a sorry conclusion. The evening, in many ways, has been like a rich fruitcake full of plums and raisins and surprises and delights, and I don't want to take up your time much more tonight, because I know many of you have to catch a bus, but I would, before we finish, like to formally thank our speakers who joined us here this evening from the length and breadth of Cowdenbeath.

Each of the speakers in their very own individual and inimitable ways contributed hugely to this symposium on peace and peace issues and I'd like to thank *all* these speakers, from all of the great religions, who agreed to throw their hats into the ring tonight. And what hats they were. We had the Reverend Colin Craig of the Unitarian Church; the Reverend Scott Macleod of the Free Kirk and his very humorous discourse on *Peace, Satan and predestination;* Sister Banyard of Our Lady of the Mission in Cathcart; and Dharma-chari Jina *(Mispronouncing)* Jinaproomijna of the Western Budda faith who waxed so eloquently on the subject of Coleridge. Then there was Rabbi Hugh MacDonald of the Jewish faith, as well as *(stares at page)* our Muslim representative and our Hindu representative whose names, if you pardon me, I will not try to reproduce at this particular juncture, all of whom showed, in their very own inimitable ways, that each and every one of us desires peace from the respective bottoms of our hearts.

And nor is the peace of God, the peace that passeth all understanding, a monopoly of the religions. We had, of course, Mr. David Brunswick, who spoke so movingly on the subject of *Peace through aromatherapy.* And we heard from our humanist and atheist friend, Miss Linda Balsam, an atheist in name certainly, but to me at least, I could very much appreciate what she had to say, just as I'm sure she could very much appreciate what *I* have to say. We also heard from Mr. Nino Caltinasetta of the Yellow December organisation who seeks, in Mr. Caltinasetta's own words, *peace on earth through direct action.* And although some of us might disagree with some of the *practical* applications, ermm even *violent* applications, of Mr. Caltinasetta's creed.... (Some of us might *not* but some of us *might* and that, of course, is all *right*. To disagree.... Or agree....) And some of our speakers *did* suggest, sad though it may be, that there *might* be occasions when violence *does* have to rear its ugly head, as Jesus did when he said that he came not to bring peace but a sword, although Jesus did *imply* on other occasions, as did some of our speakers, that complete *pacifism* was the only way to peace, eh.... *(He has lost his thread)*

But despite certain superficial disagreements, all of our speakers were passionately united in their commitment to peace. Finally, I would also have liked to have thanked Mr. Fairweather, that bright and breezy presence from the spiritualist church for all the years he's contributed so much to these events. And I'm sure I would have thanked that bright and breezy presence this year had he sadly not collapsed and died on the golf course last April. A marvellous father, a keen golfer and a skilled dentist, his passing leaves us all with a profound sense of loss. But I hope that somehow, he has managed, in his own inimitable fashion, to take back to the spirit world, much of what *we* gained from this evening's activities.

Finally again, I would like to thank you the audience. For if you, the audience, had not been here, to whom would the

speakers have spoken? Well, yes, obviously to one another - and this is, very evidently, not without value *per se*. Speaking to one another is the essence of peace and we share this essence of peace no matter our creed or religion, whether through non-violent means or otherwise, and it is this belief, coupled with the fact that we all believe in the one God, even though we may not believe in God *per se*, it is this which....
(He has lost his thread again.)

Because at the end of the day, and it is getting late, and I must conclude because I know many of you have to catch a bus, at the end of the day it is an extraordinary thing, and this is my point, that we, whether man or woman, or woman and man, because we mustn't always put the cart before the horse, whether woman or man, black or white, alive or dead, like poor Mr. Fairweather for example, can *communicate* with one another. That I, or you, or anyone in this room, or anyone *outside* this room, outside this country even - or dead - can talk, on the telephone if they live outside this country, or room, can communicate with one another, with a spiritual medium even, (if they're dead), that I can talk to you, and you can talk to me, and we can *understand* one another.

So a big, heartfelt thank you to absolutely everybody.

Sarvananda

Articles

The two articles included here are comic in terms of theme rather than style and were originally written for *Urthona* magazine. *Defying the spirit of gravity* is a manifesto of sorts. The other piece was written as part of *Urthona's* series on early cultural inspirations, *First Loves.* In it I chose to celebrate my lifelong hero and Muse, William Brown.

Defying the spirit of gravity

In my bedroom in the suburbs of Glasgow, where I lived until I was twenty-three, posters of the late, great American clowns and comedians – Buster Keaton, Charlie Chaplin, Laurel and Hardy, the Marx Brothers – covered my walls. On the sloping ceiling above my bed was a large poster of W.C.Fields, another great American comic of the 1930's. His onscreen character hated children and loved strong drink and it was his huge weeping strawberry of a nose that comforted me when I woke up, or as I was drifting off to sleep. On my bookshelves were various comic classics – *Just William, The Pickwick Papers, Don Quixote,* the Molesworth books and many others. Clowns and rogues and mischief makers, buffoons and satyrs and lords of misrule were my guardians and protectors there in deepest suburbia. But what were they protecting me *from*?

> *"And when I beheld my devil, I found him serious, thorough, profound, solemn: it was the Spirit of Gravity – through him all things are ruined. One does not kill by anger but by laughter. Come, let us kill the Spirit of Gravity."* [1]

The Spirit of Gravity, which elsewhere Nietzsche calls his "arch-enemy," I take to mean that which prevents men and women from flying, that which keeps them bound to habit, to empty ritual, to convention, to the safe, the familiar and the egocentric. The Spirit of Gravity blinds us to beauty and joy. It is in this Spirit that we carry our rafts on our backs long after we've crossed the stream. Behind this heavy, solemn and ponderous Spirit lurks fear – the fear of the new, the dangerous, and the unusual. The fear of change.

---

[1] *Thus Spake Zarathustra* – Friedrich Nietzsche

Laughing Gravy

When I was at school the highlight of my week was the TV comedy, *"Monty Python's Flying Circus."* Conceived and performed by five Oxbridge graduates and a brilliant American animator, it rose to flights of delightful, anarchic, comic silliness and fantasy. The programme set out to destroy the Spirit of Gravity as embodied in suburbia, the less attractive side of parents, pompous cliché, the kind of "straight" career my schooling was preparing me for and much of the empty ritual of our lives.

> *TOASTMASTER: Gentlemen, pray silence for the President of the Society for Putting Things on Top of Other Things.*
>
> *SIR WILLIAM: I thank you gentlemen. This year has been a good one for the Society. This year our members have put more things on top of other things than ever before. But, I should warn you, this is no time for complacency. No, there are still many things, and I cannot emphasize this too strongly, NOT on top of other things. I myself, on my way here this evening, saw a thing that was not on top of another thing in any way!*
>
> *ALL: Shame!*

Much of the attraction of the programme for me was the fact that it made fun of the ponderousness of much of the current television of the time. *Monty Python's Flying Circus* was the opposite of ponderous. The sense of freedom I experienced when I watched it was encapsulated for me in Terry Gilliam's animations which were often constructed from the legs, hands and heads of figures from the Old Master paintings. Flying Davids and Venus de Milos and Whistler's mothers defying the Spirit of Gravity before your eyes.

The Python boys always denied that their work was satirical. They preferred to describe it as "silly." One of the ways that sublime silliness manifested was through a childlike delight in language. That delight is a staple of the best comedy – a delight in words, not for any solemn purpose, but for their own sake, for their sound and musicality; for the sense of pure fun they can evoke.

> SQUIFFY: Morning Squadron leader.
>
> SQUADRON LEADER: What-ho Squiffy!
>
> SQUIFFY: How was it?
>
> SQUADRON LEADER: Top hole. Bally Jerry pranged his kite right in the how's your father. Hairy blighter dicky-birdied, feathered back on his Sammy, took a waspy; flipped over his Betty Harper's and caught his can in the Bertie.
>
> SQUIFFY: Er, I'm afraid I don't quite follow you squadron leader.
>
> SQUADRON LEADER: It's perfectly ordinary banter, Squiffy. (With a little less confidence) Bally Jerry pranged his kite right in the how's your father. Hairy blighter dicky-birdied, feathered back on his Sammy, took a waspy; flipped over his Betty Harper's and caught his can in the Bertie.
>
> SQUIFFY: No, I'm afraid I'm just not understanding banter at all well today. Give us it slower.
>
> SQUADRON LEADER: Banter's not the same if you say it slower, Squiffy.

The Spirit of Gravity destroys the joy and music of words and of language in the service of pure utility. It has a similar effect upon thinking. In this extract from *"The Gay Science,"* Nietzsche does battle again with his arch-enemy:

> *"Taking Seriously" – In the great majority, the intellect is a clumsy, gloomy creaking machine that is difficult to start. They call it "taking the matter seriously" when they want to work with this machine and think well. How burdensome they must find good thinking! The lovely human beast always seems to lose its good spirits when it thinks well; it becomes "serious." "And where laughter and gaiety are*

found, thinking does not amount to anything." That is the prejudice of this serious beast against all "gay science." Well then, let us prove that this is a prejudice."

The function of comedy is to destroy. It seeks to destroy the Spirit of Gravity and thus counteract the gravitational pull of habit and ego and literalism and all the negative states which feed habit and ego and literalism. The great, anarchic comedy team, the Marx Brothers, destroyed the pomposity of wealthy socialites, the authority of teachers and generals, and the avarice of businessmen. In his 1940 film, *"The Great Dictator"* Charlie Chaplin sought to destroy the Spirit of Gravity as embodied in one of its greatest exponents, Adolf Hitler.

The classic conception of comedy, which began with Aristotle in Ancient Greece, was that the function of comedy was to be a corrective. The comic artist's purpose was to attempt to destroy the follies and vices of society in order that society might be mended. The trickster of the North American Indian tribes might perform all his daily duties and actions backwards as a corrective to behaviour which might be over imbued with the Spirit of Gravity. Comedy destroys. It burns the dead wood of our lives, enabling the green shoots of new life to spring up.

Shakespeare's *Twelfth Night* has been described as a festive comedy which "establishes the values of holiday over every day and comic license over propriety." The festive and holiday atmosphere of the play, and the elements of misrule, destroy the Spirit of Gravity. The play is set in the courts of Lady Olivia and Duke Orsino and both characters are weighed down with this troublesome Spirit. Olivia longs to keep alive her "brother's dead love" and refuses to come out of mourning. Orsino is in love with love and is consumed with a self-indulgent passion. In the course of the play the holiday atmosphere and comic spirit reveal the fruitlessness of such self-indulgence and both characters, by the end of the play, are happy to renounce their heavy shackles and embrace life.

In *Twelfth Night* the Spirit of Gravity is personified by Malvolio, Olivia's steward, "a kind of Puritan" who is self-righteous, arrogant and has a natural hostility to enjoyment. The play's clowns flaunt such self-righteousness with their drinking, dancing and singing, and construct an elaborate scheme by which Malvolio believes he is loved by Olivia. He is utterly humiliated as a consequence. By the end of the play, the Spirit of Gravity is defeated, (rather cruelly it must be said), and Malvolio strides off crying for revenge. But it's important to note that the misrule and anarchy of the play paves the way for rule and order. Two of the clowns in particular, Sir Andrew Aguecheek and Sir Toby Belch, personify the limitations of revelry and misrule. Both end up with cracked pates and bloody noses and, at one point in the play, Sir Andrew reflects on his wasted life: "I would I had bestowed that time on the tongues that I have in fencing, dancing and bear-baiting." In their drunkenness and comic licence, the clowns flout the Spirit of Gravity as personified by the Puritan, Malvolio, but they too are weighed down by the Spirit of Gravity, (all that food and drink takes a heavy toll), and are thus rendered ridiculous themselves. It's with a slight shudder now that I recall myself staring up at the strawberry nose of W.C. Fields in my bedroom. As guardian angels, lords of misrule have limitations.

Yet I think very many of the comic novels I've read or the comic plays and films I've seen have had a purifying and benign effect on me. Perhaps it's because they've helped me to clearly see the absurdity, and the consequences, of negative mental states, particularly fear. For it is fear, the fear of breaking out of the safe, the familiar and the habitual which gives weight to the Spirit of Gravity.

In *The Religion of Art* my teacher, Sangharakshita, states that "the fundamental Buddhist state of mind is not one of fear but complete freedom from fear." Fear of God is thus a hindrance to anyone who wishes to grow spiritually. Sangharakshita goes on to say that:

"The fear of the Lord is, according to Buddhism, not the beginning of wisdom but the crown of folly. True wisdom cannot be attained until fear in all its forms has been conquered. What more effective means of dissipating this particular "fear of the Lord" could there be than the delicate mockery of the Pali scriptures?".

In Umberto Eco's *The Name of the Rose,* his 1980 novel set in a 14th Century Christian monastery, the villain of the piece is ready to destroy his fellow monks, himself and his magnificent library, to prevent a certain book from falling into anybody's hands. This book is the supposedly lost second volume of *The Poetics* of Aristotle. Its theme is laughter. Towards the end of the novel the murderer attempts to justify his crimes. (The word "villein" in the following just means "peasant."):

"Laughter, for a few moments, distracts the villein from fear. But law is imposed by fear, whose true name is fear of God. This book could strike the Luciferine spark that would set a new fire to the whole world, and laughter could be defined as the new art, unknown even to Prometheus, for cancelling fear. To the villein who laughs, at that moment, dying does not matter: but then, when the license is past, the liturgy again imposes on him, according to the divine plan, the fear of death. And from this book there could be born the new destructive aim to destroy death through redemption from fear. And what would we be, we sinful creatures, without fear, perhaps the most foresighted, the most loving of the divine gifts."

Comedy and laughter can be very useful weapons in the armoury of anyone committed to a spiritual life. The Spirit of Gravity, whether it is perceived within or without, is the arch-enemy of any such life. The Spirit of Gravity consists in ingrained habit, the stiflingly familiar, empty rites and rituals, religiosity, dogmatic opinions, self-obsession, literalism and fear of authority. Comedy, too often seen as Tragedy's younger, idiot brother, defies that Spirit of Gravity. It gives us wings.

I rest my case.

First loves: Just William

The first William book I ever read had belonged to my mother. It was William book number 13 and was called *William's Crowded Hours.* In this particular volume, amongst other things, William tries to sell his hair to a barber, takes revenge on an appalling history teacher and attempts to realise his vocation as a tramp

One of the great treats of my childhood was visiting the local library to select a William title from the ones on display: *William the Outlaw; William the Pirate; William the Rebel; Sweet William; William the Conqueror; William in Trouble....* I used to thrill to the sight of those gorgeous, colourful hardbacks wrapped in their protective plastic covers. Occasionally I would fork out 3/6 from my pocket money to buy a William book of my own. The marvellous illustrations by Thomas Henry captured the anarchic splendour of the books and were often very funny in themselves: here was William with his tousled hair and intense stare, intimidating a nervous visitor to the village; here were William, Henry, Douglas and Ginger, *The Outlaws,* being chased across a field by the incensed Farmer Jenks; here was Jumble, William's mongrel dog, dancing by William's side....

William breathed the spirit of the outdoors, of glorious Saturdays. Other heroes like Jennings and Billy Bunter were never quite in William's league. He was the boy I wanted to be. I looked upon William with hero worship and with an awe which sometimes bordered on fear. For William's optimism and confidence were fierce and he could be quite solemn, even challenging, in his pursuit of adventure:

> *"Anythin' might turn up," said William. "Gosh! There mus' be things turnin' up all over the place. You've only got to find 'em. You don't jus' sit waitin' for 'em. I bet people like King Arthur an' Boadicea an' - an' Dick Turpin an' Robin*

Hood didn't jus' sit around waitin' for things to turn up. They went out an' found 'em..."

Richmal Crompton wrote her first William story just after the end of the First World War. She was still writing about "that little savage" on the day before she died in January 1969. In those fifty years William's world essentially changed very little. His un-named village remained largely insulated from world events. And although certain of his enthusiasms waxed and waned with the times, William too stayed essentially the same - mischievous, supremely adventurous, anarchic but with a readily aggrieved sense of justice and a dogged determination to set things right.

In William's world there were two kinds of adult. There was the good sort, who might press a half crown into William's hand for getting rid of a troublesome relative or providing some hilarious diversion. And then there were those unfortunate adults who became William's foils and victims - the pompous and the pretentious and the incurably serious. Such unfortunates included the dreadful Botts of Botts Hall, the *nouveaux riches* of William's village. (The Botts had a ghastly daughter, Violet Elizabeth, who came as close as anyone to becoming William's nemesis: "I'll thcweam and thcweam and thcweam until I'm thick.")

Other adults who suffered at William's hands included his brother Robert, who was constantly meeting "the most beautiful girl in the world," his sister Ethel, and his long-suffering parents. Mrs. Brown's belief that one day her son would become a normal, clean, well-behaved boy was pathetically touching but utterly deluded. William's family could just not comprehend William's behaviour. And his family's behaviour seemed utterly incomprehensible to William. This was particularly true of his brother and sister's frequent habit of falling in love. This basically baffled William and his meddling in his brother and sister's affairs of the heart led to many farcical and painful incidents.

Not that William himself was entirely immune to love. Every hero has an Achilles heel and William's particular Achilles heel came in the form of a little girl called Joan who had dark hair and dimples. Admittedly, Joan was happy to join in The Outlaws' games of pirates and Red Indians and, as girls went, she wasn't too bad, but I didn't like to see my hero blushing or tongue tied. The stories which featured Joan made me a little uncomfortable.

But such fallings-away on the part of my hero were rare. William's confidence, resourcefulness and sense of freedom were seldom seriously compromised. William was my role model. He showed me how a boy should behave, (in his imagination at least), and he rarely let me down.

I don't generally re-visit the books I read as a child but, such was Richmal Crompton's comic gift, I can still read the William stories with genuine enjoyment. They are very well written, skilfully plotted and extremely funny. I suspect that everything I write or have ever written is somehow influenced by Richmal Crompton's writing and by what she came to call her "Frankenstein's monster," William Brown. And maybe that's not such a bad thing.

Sarvananda

Fictional autobiography

I can't write straight memoir or autobiography. I'm not sure why. It all tends to emerge rather stilted and superficial. It seems that, in order to write about my life, I need to retain a certain distance from it, to mythologise my experience, to have the permission to be unfair, inconsiderate and rude. While, at the same time, not journeying *too* far from my actual experience.

Included under this heading are sections from *Lawrence of Suburbia*, an abandoned semi-autobiographical novel, abandoned because it just kept growing and growing. The material is already beginning to surface in other forms so nothing is really wasted. I have a strong commitment, as a writer, to saving resources and all my unused jokes do tend to get recycled.

From Lawrence of Suburbia

The horrors

Not long after Uncle Ron was killed, my goldfish died. This was the second death in so many months. Brian was the only pet I've had before or since. We flushed him down the toilet. I seemed to be more upset about Brian than I was about Uncle Ron but I think I was just as upset about Uncle Ron, probably even more so. One night I dreamt that Uncle Ron was splashing about in a huge toilet bowl and there was a flushing noise, and Uncle Ron went round and round and disappeared, and I woke up screaming. That night Mummy took me into bed with her and Daddy. Mummy held on to me very tightly indeed, so tightly that it almost hurt.

I began to have regular nightmares and insisted that the hall light be left on and my bedroom door be left half open. I would try my best to stay awake, so that I wouldn't have the nightmares. But then, I would become aware of the beating of my own heart. If my heart stopped beating, I realised, I would die. Knowing this, my heart beat faster which made me convinced I was having a heart attack and this, of course, made me even more worried and made my heart beat faster still.[2]

Every evening now, before I finally dropped off to sleep, I vividly imagined all the different ways I could die, or be badly damaged. I could be bitten by a mad dog and get rabies. I could get mugged, thrown to the ground, knock my head on the pavement and go into a coma. I could get run over. I

---

[2] 2020 records show that the number of children under the age of nine to die from a heart attack in the calendar year 1962 are almost negligible. Unfortunately, I was unaware of these statistics at the time.

could fall asleep in the bath and drown. I could sleepwalk, open the kitchen cabinet and take a mouthful of whatever was in that strangely alluring dark blue bottle marked POISON. I could choke on my tongue. I could get buried in the Blackwater graveyard and wake up to find that I wasn't dead and not be able to claw my way out of the coffin. I could be bitten by a poisonous spider. I could get electrocuted by the toaster. A plastic bag, one of those that said DANGER OF SUFFOCATION, could find its way over my face and I could suffocate. I could be crushed by a cupboard or by heavy shelves. I could drown in the swimming baths. I could somehow get locked in the school cloakroom, just before the holidays and starve to death. I could get a terrible disease of which there were many. I could be struck on the head by a golf ball and get brain damage and become a vegetable. All these fears and anxieties became known as my "horrors." It was my father's phrase.

"Had the horrors again last night old boy?" he'd ask kindly as I stumbled into the kitchen for *Rice Crispies*, toast and sympathy.

After my bath, and just before she and I went upstairs for the evening ritual and prayer, my mother, with infinite patience, would address my barrage of *what ifs*.

"What if I choke on a peanut?"

"You won't choke on a peanut, dear."

"How do you know I won't?"

"Because you chew your food carefully."

"No, I don't. You're always telling me to eat more slowly and carefully."

I stood in front of the fire, wrapped in a great bath towel while Mummy exhibiting her uncanny ability to multi-task, vigorously rubbed me dry, examined my nails, teeth and crevices and responded to my anxieties.

"I tell you to chew your food carefully just in *case*."

"Just in case I choke."

"You won't choke. And Daddy and me are always here to thump you on the back."

"That's right," said Daddy.

Daddy was usually there as well, although he didn't contribute a lot to the conversation. He'd sit in his armchair smoking and the smoke would drift down his nostrils and sometimes he'd put more coal on the fire. My Dad was in Missing Persons and, after putting in a full day talking to the relatives of the missing persons, or supervising the dragging of ponds, he was happy to leave most of the evening's work to Beryl.

"Thumping me on the back might not work," I told Beryl. "It might be too late. You might not be able to *dislodge* the peanut."

"What's all this about peanuts, dear?" asked my mother, exploring my ear with a cotton bud, ever vigilant for wax. "You don't even like peanuts very much. I can't remember when you last had a peanut."

"We have them when visitors come. And I was just using that as an example. It could be a *Malteser* or anything."

"It's no use worrying about it, Lawrence."

"But I do worry about it."

"Worrying doesn't help. Anyway, just chew your food carefully and there won't be a problem."

"What if I forget?"

"You won't forget."

"I do forget."

"Well, you haven't choked yet, dear."

"There's always a first time. That's what you keep saying. 'There's always a first time for everything.'".

"It's pointless worrying about it, Lawrence. It's not going to happen. Now get into your pyjamas."

The conversation was suspended briefly as the towel was removed and I was helped into my pyjamas.

"You once choked on a fish bone," I resumed.

"That's why I always take the bones out the fish these days. We don't have fish with bones."

"But we have *Maltesers*."

"*Maltesers* don't have bones."

"But they're small. Like peanuts. You can choke on them."

"Lawrence darling, you can worry about anything. You can worry that the ceiling might fall in. But it's not going to happen."

But I wasn't so sure. I gazed doubtfully up at the ceiling and imagined a scenario where cupboards and chairs and the double bed, with Mummy and Daddy in it, and the dressing table and the whole caboodle, came crashing into the living room in clouds of dust to the sounds of splintering wood and cascading plaster and the horrified screams of my parents.

And I imagined the aftermath with the police chief gazing sorrowfully at the newly orphaned little boy.

"I'm sorry, son. The floorboards were rotten to the core."

And a tearful Mrs. Savage from next door putting an arm around my shoulders as the dead bodies of my parents, covered in grey blankets, were taken out to the ambulance on stretchers.

Eventually the horrors got so bad that I was given a spoonful, every evening before bed, of what became known as my "Worry Bottle." This was a pink, gooey, tranquillising medicine which tasted of sour bubble-gum. Good God, I can taste it still as I write.

William and I almost burn the house down

One afternoon William and I were playing in the good room, the cold and slightly unloved room, typical of every suburban home in Blackwater, which was reserved for visitors and special occasions. In the middle of a game of *Risk*, William got some matches from his pocket.

"Light that candle, Lawrence," he said, pointing to a long dinner candle which sat in a little alcove.

"We never light that candle," I said. "And I'm not allowed to play with matches. You know that."

"I've got a trick," said William. "Duncan showed me. Quick, or I'll lose the chance…"

He spoke with a sense of urgency and when William was this enthusiastic about something, he was impossible to resist. So, despite grave misgivings, I took the matches, lit the dinner candle and held it next to him at waist height, as he'd asked. If I'd known what was going to happen, of course, I would have made sure the candle was not close to anything flammable.

It all happened very quickly. William bent over the candle flame, frowned with concentration and fired off an enormous fart. This produced a spectacular sheet of blue flame which immediately ignited the net curtains. I screamed and dropped the candle on to the rug and William screamed and we both ran out of the good room and into the living room where poor Sid was trying to catch forty winks in front of the telly after a busy week searching for the missing people of Glasgow and environs.

"The house is on fire!" I screamed.

Sid ran into the good room and stamped out the flames on the rug and then beat the flaming curtains out with the other rug and threw a vase of water over the sofa, which was also threatening to ignite.

I managed to stay unusually calm during the subsequent grilling. Despite my mother's tight-lipped fury, despite my father's police training, I managed to stick to my story. For I knew, if William was in any way implicated, I wouldn't be able to see him for a long time. So, I took the rap.

I said I had lit a candle for Jesus and dropped it.

My parents were very suspicious, especially Beryl. I could tell that she thought that William was somehow responsible. But I wouldn't budge and William backed me up.

"Never, never, never, *never* play with fire," said my mother.

"Sorry," I said. "It will never happen again."

As it was, I wasn't allowed to play with William for two weeks and, for the next fortnight, the acrid stink of my sin followed me around the house. I had told a terrible lie and I was even tempted to confess. But I wasn't prepared not to see William for a long, long time. Two weeks was bad enough. And my Mum and Dad had promised a while ago that William could come on holiday with us. If I'd told the truth, viz. William had set fire to the good room with a lit fart, he'd never be allowed to come.

So, I just had to put up with being a bad sheep for a while and William came on holiday with us.

By the way, a note to any younger readers: Do not practice lighting your farts at home without a responsible adult present.

Coming out

To Mark Slade c/o NBC studios, Burbank, California, USA.

Dear Mark Slade,

My name is Lawrence, I am fifteen years old and I live in Glasgow, Scotland, UK. I just wanted to write to say how much I enjoy your performance as Billy "Blue" Cannon in *The High Chapparal* which is, in my opinion, the best Western series on TV, easily outranking *The Virginian* and *Bonanza*, for example. Coincidentally, I have a friend called Blue who looks quite like you and with whom I am in love. (I think I might be gay.)

I hope you are well and thanks again for some very enjoyable moments. I enclose a stamped addressed air-mail envelope if you wish to reply.

Sincerely,

Lawrence Lawrence.

(Lawrence is both my first and last name.)

P.S. I hope to be an actor myself one day.

To Lawrence Lawrence, 41 Blackwater Avenue, Glasgow, Scotland.

Dear Lawrence,

Thank you very much for your letter and I'm glad you enjoy *The High Chapparal*. I enclose a signed photograph. Hang on to it. It may be very valuable one day! With very best wishes for the future,

Mark Slade

Lying on the old dam wall

I had my first vision here. At this bend in the river, next to the old, ruined mill. It was also the scene of that infamous childhood transgression when I swam with William McCorkadale, me in my blue Y fronts and he in his Bugs Bunny briefs. It was here that I had my first can of beer and here that I had my first cigarette. If you happen to be sitting on the remains of the dam wall, if you sort of topple backwards and crane your neck, you can just make out a squat, ugly building of red brick on the Castlemilk side of the river. It was in that public convenience that I had intimate communion with the married, the lonely, the curious, the closeted, the too unattractive, the too old, the too young, the bisexual, the plain horny and the occasional visitor who had, in all innocence, come in to urinate and had got more than he bargained for.

It was here, in 1820, when they were digging the foundations for the mill, that they found a flint tool and a flint arrowhead. Nearby, in what is now Blackwater Crescent, there's evidence to suggest that there was a settlement with thirty houses, each with a sunken chamber. Think of that, a little wetlands community in Blackwater three thousand years before I was born. I find that comforting. So, when I lie on the dam wall, I reflect that there were people here, by the river, before Miss Creake and her tawse, before rolling news, before Josef Stalin and Attila the Hun and bloody Jesus on his bloody cross. Before Yahweh, the Old Testament War God, there were people here worshipping gods of their own. Before all the screaming hullaballoo, there were people here, in the good old days, when all you had to worry about was bears, starvation and being wiped out by a neighbouring settlement.

And perhaps a boy came down here regularly to be alone, a coward, a Mummy's boy, a bit of a shaman. Perhaps he ate some of the wetland mushrooms here and lay down and had visions.

Grandad in a box

I was becoming increasingly worried over religious matters. Did I love Jesus? Did I want to give my heart to him? And how did certain experiences that I'd had connect with Jesus and God and religion? That figure in red, for example, whom I'd dreamt about.... Was that the Devil? Had I seen the Devil? And what had happened that afternoon after I'd left the history class? Had I seen God that afternoon? Or was I going mad?

I didn't seek the answers to these questions amongst immediate family members. I had a sense I'd be disappointed. Once, Sid had come home after a police dinner, a bit worse for wear, and had sat down heavily next to me on the couch as I was watching the late-night film, a pretty sub-standard Hammer horror. As the film came to a close and various Christian artefacts were brandished in front of Christopher Lee, I took advantage of my Dad's inebriated state, to ask a serious question.

"You think there's a God, Dad?"

"I don't even know how the central heating works," said my father. "Ask your Mum."

To be fair, I had caught him at a bad moment, and he must have remembered the conversation, because a couple of days later, *apropos* of nothing at all, he declared to me that life was a very mysterious affair and certain things could only be explained by the fact that there was a God.

"Why, for example," he said, "do men have nipples?"

I wasn't sure how the fact that men had nipples proved the existence of God, but I didn't pursue it. I didn't share my religious concerns with my mother because I didn't want to share *any* of my worries with my mother at that time. I did consider talking to Grandad Sinclair but I wasn't sure where he stood on the Devil and feared, perhaps unfairly, that his response to any of my questions might prove to be lacking in substance. In any event, a possible conversation was precluded by the fact that Grandad became very ill. He moved in with us permanently so Beryl, my mother, could look after him. Soon he was starting to spend most of his time in bed and a flow of nurses and visitors began to call at the house.

"Is Grandad going to get better?" I asked Beryl one day.

She gave a little shake of her head.

I didn't want Grandad to die. He'd always been pretty dour, short-tempered and annoying, but I was basically fond of him and I knew he was fond of me. Some afternoons, if I was passing the bowling-green, I would go and sit on one of the benches and watch him playing bowls with his friends. I think he enjoyed that. He always gave me a wave and sometimes he'd sit on the bench next to me and give me a *Polo* mint and ask how I'd got on at school that day.

Soon there was a nurse in the house full-time.

"Won't be long now, Lawrence," said my mother. She looked incredibly sad and there were dark circles under her eyes. She'd been staying up with Grandad most of the night.

Later that day, my mother told me that Grandad would like to see me. Mum ushered me into his bedroom which was too hot and had an unpleasant smell. My Aunt Dorothy was sitting by Grandad's bed and a nurse was removing a bowl which I made a point of not examining as she carried it out of the room. Grandad's head seemed to be disappearing into the pillow. His skin was yellow, his cheeks sunken and he made a whistling noise every time he took a breath. He seemed to have shrunk in size since I'd seen him last week. I felt scared and looked to my mother for some kind of guidance.

"Your Grandad wants to tell you something," said Beryl.

Hesitantly, I went over to Grandad's bed. His eyes were wide and staring. His lips moved slightly and I bent down to catch what he might be saying. His breath smelt surprisingly sweet. I couldn't hear him. I bent down further.

"Look after your teeth, son," whispered Grandad.

Grandad died later that night and there was a funeral about a week later. Beryl thought that I was too young to go to the funeral but I surprised myself by insisting that I go, although this entailed buying a suit. We got a suit that was too big for me, my mother reasoning that, as I had some way to go yet in the next couple of years in terms of physical development, she didn't want to have to buy another suit in a year's time and that I would soon grow into it.

And so, I sat, manipulating the cuffs of my new suit, in the front row of the Blackwater Crematorium chapel, along with the immediate family: my mother, my father, my Aunt Dorothy, my Aunt Rose and my Uncle Brian. I felt very self-conscious. I was unsure how to behave, or even how to feel. The organist played some sombre music and my mother, who was sitting next to me, snuffled a bit. I was terrified she'd take my hand. Then the pall bearers from the Co-op carried in the coffin and laid it on the trestle beneath a large, silver crucifix. They then bowed their heads briefly, the palm of one hand covering the back of the other. I noticed that one of the men had tattoos on his knuckles. The pall bearers retired and the Minister stood up, but he gave us a minute to take in Grandad. Grandad in a box. Where it all ends, a wooden box, just big enough to lie in but not big enough to light a cigarette, or read a newspaper. And there he was, in his box, grumpy Grandad Sinclair who was, I suspect, not totally reconciled to being dead. And I imagined a muffled, irascible voice emanating from the depths of that box.

"Beryl, there's not enough room to swing a *cat* in here."

A certain hysteria began to rise in my throat. I was going to laugh. I'm sure it was nerves but it wasn't just nerves. It was the joy of being alive and not being in a box, not trapped, like

Laughing Gravy

Grandad, without even a *Polo* mint to help him on his way. I put my head in my hands and made a barking sound which everyone surely translated as grief.

Well, they wouldn't have been *entirely* mistaken.

Sarvananda

Poems and lyrics

I don't write poetry as a rule but I wanted to include something from way back, a "coming out" poem which I wrote in 1982. The other pieces in this section are song lyrics. My friend Satyadaka and I wrote about forty songs over lockdown and I found I had a certain talent for coming up with melodies - which was a pleasant surprise. The songs incorporated a variety of moods and styles but the lyrics I've included here are comic in tone. *Toad* was inspired by Philip Larkin's poem. The lyrics to *Strange things happen to me* were written by both myself and Satyadaka.

A cautionary tale of Tom, who denied his own nature and became a vegetable

On a dark and fateful day in May,
Tom told his parents he was gay.
His mother shrieked; his father scolded.
(His grand-dad's pacemaker exploded.)
'Oh God!' roared dad, 'Our son's a pansy!
A fag! a fruit! a queer! a Nancy!

Oh, tell me, God, what have we done
to merit such cruelty from our son?
My lad,' said he, 'you've quite appalled
your grand-dad, me, and most of all –
your mother, who most painfully bore you.
Tom, for our sakes, I implore you…
Go and see a doctor, *please*.
He'll cure you of this vile disease.'

So next day they took Tom to see
Doctor Tuffnell Williams MBE,
a man renowned throughout the land
for treating sexual deviants.

Laughing Gravy

'Doc,' said Dad, 'our son's a bender:
He fancies those of his own gender.
So, make him normal, if you can,
and we'll make you a wealthy man.'

So, Dr Williams set about
trying to get Tom straightened out.
At first, he tried to cure Tom's ills
by filling him full of hormone pills –
to no avail. So, then he jabbed him,
poked him, pricked him, pierced him, stabbed him.
But no response. Tom got much worse.
He'd fallen for a cute male nurse
called Kenny, who had lovely dimples,
and a dial entirely free from pimples.

Ken loved Tom too. What bliss! What joy!
True love requited! Boy loves Boy!
So, one night Ken and Tom eloped,
using bed-sheets for a rope.
They fled by boat across the sea
and set up house quite near Portree
in a little cottage. Oh, what bliss!
There they'd cuddle, smooch and kiss,
and do the things that can't be done
under the age of 21.

Sarvananda

Those happy days continued, till
down from the farm and over the hill
came the farmer's son, one Dhonald Maclay,
and he stole the heart of Ken away!
Oh, fickle youth! Tom's love Ken spurned –
and all for a smile, and a large milk-churn!
Not caring whether he lived or died,
Tom forever left the shores of Skye,
and on the mainland went to see
Doctor Tuffnell Williams, MBE,
and sadly said, 'Now listen, Tuff,
make me normal – I've had enough.'

So, after a course of sixteen talks
on the joys of marriage, and electric shocks,
and little tablets for his genes,
and pornographic magazines –
Tom was cured. (So, Tufnell said.)
And two years later, Tom was wed.
His parents were both overjoyed
that he'd married a girl and not a boy:
'And Mabel's such a lovely wife:
She'll see to him – she'll change his life.'

And they were right, for very soon her
fruitful womb bore Tuffnell Junior.
But Tom ignored his little boy.

Laughing Gravy

His heart was closed to every joy.
He rarely smiled – just watched the telly,
ate KP nuts, and saw his belly
grow and grow, till very soon
it had grown to the size of a barrage balloon.

Now and then, on a Saturday night,
he'd wander the streets, and perhaps he might
visit a cottage (alas; not in Skye)
and find, perhaps, a lonely guy
like him. But Mabel stopped all that,
and Tom grew silent, moped and sat
chewing his nuts, grew fatter still,
ate, moped, and grew, and grew, until
with a loud report TOM'S BELLY BURST,
filling the house with a cold, grey dust.

'He never had time to say "Beg your pardon",'
wept Mabel as they buried him in the garden.
And in that garden every year
carrots, beans and sprouts appear
where Tom was buried. There you'll find
vegetables of every kind.

Moral

My poem's done. The ending's sad.

Sarvananda

But can't we be both gay *and* glad?

It can be so, (it's up to you),

if to yourself you remain true.

Published in "Gay Scotland" – 1982

Selkie

What are whiskers and flippers to you?
And what are flippers to me?
And why do I sigh when I hear the cry –
The cry and the call of the sea?

God's plan is that man is a man is a man
And he isnae a fish or an eel.
But I ken in my heart that I'm set apart.
I'm half seal.

Selkie! Selkie!
A selkie's life is free, (is free)!
Selkie! Selkie!
A selkie's life for me!

I've worked an age for the minimum wage –
A drone and a boring landlubber.
Oh, what a hoot to change my suit
Into one of natural blubber!

A selkie's a creature half human, half seal
And it sings a glorious song.
In a quiet wee bay, I could frolic and play
All day long.

Sarvananda

Selkie! Selkie!

A selkie's life is free, (is free)!

Selkie! Selkie!

A selkie's life for me!

Some people insist it doesnae exist,

That a selkie is simply a myth.

But a myth is a thing with a wonderful ring

When you're feeling stuck fast on the earth.

So noo and again when the world of men

Has me feelin a' wrong in my skin,

I'll go doon to the sea, reveal the true me

And just dive in.

Selkie! Selkie!

A selkie's life is free, (is free)!

Selkie! Selkie!

A selkie's life for me!

Fine thanks

Frankenstein's monster took the train

To see a specialist about his brain.

The doc said, "Mate, your brain is broke.

I'm afraid you're going to croak."

Oh dear! Oh, dearie me!

He went off on a killing spree.

But when his wife asked "How'd your day go?"

This is what the monster said, (oh)

(Oh) Fine thanks.

Just fine thanks.

Had a great time.

And I'm feeling really fine.

Fine thanks.

Just fine thanks.

I'm just tickety boo.

It was my Uncle Rodney's fate

To fall from the top of the Empire State

At each of more than fifty floors

He tipped his hat to the folk indoors.

Sarvananda

Oh dear! Oh, dearie me!
My uncle won't be back for tea!
But when he reached floor 32
A lady called "How do you do?"
(And my uncle said)

Fine thanks.
Just fine thanks.
I'm feeling really fine.
This happens all the time.
Fine thanks.
Just fine thanks.
I'm just tickety boo.

We hit an iceberg on a cruise.
The water spoiled my brand new shoes.
But the band played on as the ship went down
And we danced away to the big band sound.

Oh dear! Oh, dearie me!
The ship's going down in the cold, cold sea.
But when Maestro asked us all
How were we enjoying the ball
(We said)

Fine thanks.
Just fine thanks.

Laughing Gravy

Everything is fine

And the music is divine.

Fine thanks.

Just fine thanks.

We're just tickety boo.

I'm just tickety

We're just tickety

Everything is tickety boo!

Strange things happen to me

When I was a lad about so high
(Strange things happen to me.)
I saw an angel in the sky
(Strange things happen to me.)

Then down-and-out and on the dole
(Strange things happen to me.)
I saw God's face in my cereal bowl
(Strange things happen to me.)

Angelic Chorus:
And he will play in the heavenly band
And he will sail for the Holy Land
It just won't happen the way he planned.
Strange things happen to him.

I got a job in Liberty Hall
(Strange things happen to me.)
One day I walked right through a wall
(Strange things happen to me.)

When I was middle-aged and broke
(Strange things happen to me.)
I saved the life of another bloke

Laughing Gravy

(Strange things happen to me.)

Broken hearted, mad with wine,
(Strange things happen to me.)
I was kissed by the Devil on the Circle Line.
(Strange things happen to me.)

Angelic Chorus:
And he will play in the heavenly band
And he will sail for the Holy Land
It just won't happen the way he planned.
Strange things happen to him.

My back is bent, my hair is grey
(Strange things happen to me.)
I laugh and dance all through the day
(Strange things happen to me.)

I couldn't ask for anything more
(Strange things happen to me.)
I'm standing at an open door
(Strange things happen to me.)

Angelic Chorus:
And he will play in the heavenly band
And he will sail for the Holy Land
It just won't happen the way he planned.

Sarvananda

Strange things happen to him.

(Lyrics Sarvananda and Satyadaka)

Toad

The day was sunny, bright and still.
I phoned in work, said I was ill.
I left the house, went on my way
To fly a kite, enjoy the day
But there, half way down Cemetery Road,
I came across a massive toad
Who said to me,
"Hey, shouldn't you be working?"

Toad, toad -
Working nine to five.
Toad, toad -
Squatting on my life.
Toad, toad –
Fat face full of sorrow.
You were there yesterday.
And you'll be there tomorrow.

They locked us down, said "Do not roam.
Turn on the lap top. Work from home"
"Bugger this. I beg your pardon.
I'll take time off in the garden."
But underneath my cherry tree
Two beady eyes were watching me.

Sarvananda

As if to say,
"Hey, shouldn't you be working?"

Toad, toad -
Working nine to five.
Toad, toad -
Squatting on my life.
Toad, toad –
Fat face full of sorrow.
You were there yesterday.
And you'll be there tomorrow.

At the age of sixty-one
I resigned from *Mathew and Son*
To do the things I'd never done,
To write the novel not begun.
(But) I'd only reached page twenty-six
When a deadly, poisoned kiss
Turned my handsome Prince
Into a toad.

Toad, toad -
Working nine to five.
Toad, toad -
Squatting on my life.
Toad, toad –
Fat face full of sorrow.

Laughing Gravy

You were there yesterday.

And you'll be there tomorrow.

Sarvananda

Final words

And finally, three pieces written especially for this anthology. I don't know where Indestructible Bob came from. He woke me up one night and demanded to have the final word, so I obliged.

Famous last words

Have you ever thought what your last words might be? I think it's something worth reflecting on. This is especially so if your life hasn't amounted to much. If your life *hasn't* amounted to much, but you manage to say something memorable on your death bed, you might very well redeem yourself, at the very last minute, in the eyes of the world. Even if your life has been relatively successful, it's good to go out with a bang. So here are some tips which you may find useful in considering your last words.

Plan your last words in advance.

Don't rely on spontaneity as you are breathing your last. Plan your last words well in advance, and we're talking about months or even years ahead because who knows when your time will come. Scrabbling around on your death bed, trying to come up with a memorable phrase may appear undignified and will, more often than not, be fruitless.

Memorise your last words.

Commit your last words to memory. When it is time to die your mind might feel a bit foggy or you may be anxious and preoccupied. So, it is necessary to have your last words at your beck and call and readily available for utterance at the appointed time. Otherwise, your last words might be anti-climactic, at best. Do you really want to exit this world to the phrase "That nut roast tasted a bit off," or, "I have a pig of a headache"?

Write your last words down.

Another good tip is to write your last words down on a piece of paper and keep the piece of paper in a safe place and to hand. Then, as you are dying, if despite your best efforts, you're unable to recall your last words, you can ask a loved one to retrieve the piece of paper and hand it to you so that you can proclaim your last message to the world with dignity and confidence.

Should I appoint a surrogate?

Although it is always useful to have a surrogate ready to read your last words, (in case of verbal impairment for example), I would not use one personally if I could possibly avoid it. Using a surrogate takes the spotlight away from *you*. Also, a surrogate has less invested in getting things right. A friend of mine appointed a surrogate after losing the power of speech. Unfortunately, the surrogate in question could not read my friend's hand writing and instead of saying, "Goodbye, I leave for a better place," said, "Goodbye, I leave with a bitter face." This did not strike the appropriate valedictory note at all.

Don't necessarily wait until the very moment of death to deliver your last words

If you are still a bit worried about declaiming your last words effectively and appropriately on your death bed, you can always convey them during the dying process when you still have the confidence and capacity to articulate clearly. You can even announce your last words as soon as you are given a terminal diagnosis. However, once you've uttered your last words, it's best to remain silent and not say anything else until you actually die.

Be brief.

Keep your last words short and simple. Don't try and thank everybody, for example. You are not accepting an Oscar. Brevity is also a great boon when faced with *sudden* death. If a bus is bearing down upon you, a Shakespearian soliloquy is quite useless but a very brief aphorism, (uttered very loudly, in order that bystanders might hear), may propel you towards posthumous celebrity status. A Mrs. Lydia Hunter of Aberdeen made the local news after falling to her death from some scaffolding. During her rapid descent she found the presence of mind to bellow Edith Piaf's immortal line "Je ne regrette rien" (I have no regrets) – and received a standing ovation in the process from the admiring bystanders.

What about the content of your last words?

What should you actually convey with your last words? Should your last words be poetic? Moving? Heroic? Not necessarily. They can even be slightly self-effacing. Not content with writing, in his own death notice in *The Times*, that he had just *"conked out,"* the actor John Le Mesurier, before he slipped into a coma, declared: "It's all been rather lovely." The important thing is that your last words, like those of Mr. Le Mesurier, should be *memorable* and that you should present yourself in as interesting and attractive a light as possible.

Be yourself.

Make your last word appropriate to *you*. A cousin of mine signed off with Nelson's famous phrase "Kiss me, Hardy." Although this had the advantage of being brief (see above), it was very inappropriate in the circumstances, the circumstances being that he had fallen out of the back of a Land Rover in Blairgowrie Safari Park and was being mauled by lions. It is possible that my cousin was being amusing and ironic but who knows. Irony is a difficult thing to convey when you are dying.

Enjoy yourself.

This will be your last chance to present yourself in a good and favourable light. You will be more able to convey all this if you *enjoy* your moment in the spotlight and, as much as possible given the circumstances, relish the opportunity to shine.

Apocalypse the noo

Apocalypse: noun

1. A very serious event resulting in great destruction and change.

2. The end of the world

3. A spiritual revelation or disclosure.

Ironically enough, it wasn't climate change or war, nuclear or otherwise, that did for the planet in the end. It was an asteroid, a massive, great brute of a thing, about two hundred times bigger than the asteroid that killed off the dinosaurs after it fell on the town of Chicxulub in Mexico, about 66 million years ago, round about lunch time.

We weren't given much warning about the asteroid which killed us all - only about a week. During that week there was much debate as to why the astronomers hadn't seen it coming, and why there had been so little warning. The astronomers countered that their various governments had asked them not to publicise the fact that there was an asteroid hurtling in our direction, as it might induce global panic. Furthermore, their figures had indicated that the asteroid would just miss the Earth. Subsequently however, as it became evident that the asteroid *would* indeed collide with Earth, the astronomers admitted that they had not considered closely enough what is called, (in scientific jargon), *The Wobble Factor.* This, strictly speaking, was a *variety* of factors including the gravitational pull of other planetary bodies in our solar system, the huge mass of the asteroid in question and sloppy arithmetic.

So yes, we only had a week to prepare for the annihilation of our home planet and this was, understandably, very stressful for many people who were unsure how to use their last days most appropriately. The people of Arbroath, in Scotland, are to be very much praised in this regard. It was announced at the beginning of our last week on Earth that Arbroath (pre-collision population 23,902) would receive the initial impact of the asteroid. Over the next forty-eight hours the people of Arbroath came together as one to beautify the town and to welcome the many visitors, members of the media and camera crews who were already beginning to arrive. Some very striking herbaceous borders were created, local residents opened their doors and provided bed and breakfast at very reasonable rates and a most impressive sign was erected on the side of the A92 road into the town which read: *WELCOME TO ARBROATH. ASTEROID CAPITAL OF THE WORLD. HOME OF THE ARBROATH SMOKIE.* (An Arbroath Smokie is a local, and particularly delicious, kind of smoked haddock.)

As our last week proceeded, many people throughout the world got a bit depressed and anxious - but it wasn't *all* glum faces by any means. Picnics, street parties, spontaneous "happenings" and communal events generally were widespread. Many people put aside racial, religious, and national differences and just enjoyed one another's company. Community singing was a great favourite with all and sundry and, towards the end of the week, a particular song went viral and became the international anthem. This was, (somewhat surprisingly), the 1984 hit, *Wake me up before you go go* by *Wham*. There was also a lot of urgent questioning regarding the meaning of life. Many of my friends used the time to deepen their spiritual practice and, generally, there was a great upsurge in spiritual awakening with a significant number of people ceasing to identify with their bodies and thoughts and instead, identifying, (if indeed, we can use that word), with the overarching, loving but impersonal awareness which unifies all sentient beings. So that was a positive. There was also much interesting discussion and light hearted badinage amongst my friends and myself as to where we all might be reborn, given that the Earth would no longer be able to sustain human life.

As predicted, the asteroid struck Arbroath about 7pm, the epicentre of the impact being Morrisons' Superstore in Hume Street. All humanity perished. Not all life became extinct, however. For example, a great many insects survived and, not too long after the event, rosebay willowherb, sometimes referred to as fireweed or bombweed, spread its luxurious pink carpets over the ruined cities and decorated the devastated remains of the White House, the Kremlin, and other celebrated buildings and monuments etc.

On a personal note, I well remember my last day on earth. My friends and I had hired a boat which we sailed up the Clyde. We had a little party and rejoiced in one another's good qualities. As the asteroid hit and the earth shuddered, we watched in awe as extraordinary rainbows illuminated the sky. And, as the tsunami which was about to kill our little party pulsed up the river, and as we all sang *Wake me up before you go go,* I could not help but be reminded of the words of the 14th Century anchorite, Lady Julian of Norwich: *"All will be well, and all will be well, and all manner of things will be well."*

Indestructible Bob

Some nasty men had it in for Indestructible Bob.

One afternoon, one of the nasty men punched Indestructible Bob on the face outside *Lidl*.

"Thank you," said Indestructible Bob as blood streamed from his nose onto his shopping.

The next day another of the nasty men tried to run Indestructible Bob over in his car but he misjudged his approach very badly and ended up going through the plateglass window of a chip shop. Indestructible Bob pulled the nasty man from the wreckage and asked the nasty man if he was all right.

"Shut up," said the nasty man who felt humiliated, as well as concussed.

A month later, yet another nasty man, positioned in an upstairs window, shot at Indestructible Bob with a SA80a2 rifle as Indestructible Bob was coming home from Bingo. The bullet missed Indestructible Bob and grazed the paw of a badger who had been foraging in Indestructible Bob's bins. Indestructible Bob, who loved animals, took the badger into his house, and administered first aid. He then befriended the badger - and man and beast became inseparable.

Three months later a group of the nasty men hid behind Indestructible Bob's privet hedge and sprang out as Indestructible Bob, (with the badger trotting behind him), came out of his house to water his plants. They assaulted Indestructible Bob with golf clubs, heavy sticks and a baseball bat. In all probability, the outcome would have been a tragic one had not the badger, with great presence of mind, scurried purposefully to the local police station and, by both tugging at the sleeves of the desk sergeant and his colleagues and making significant growling, yelping and barking noises, alerted the police to danger and led them directly to the scene of the ongoing assault. All the nasty men were taken into custody apart from the nasty man who had been pulled out of the wreckage of his car by Indestructible Bob some months previously. The nasty man who had been pulled out of the wreckage of his car by Indestructible Bob some months previously managed to run away and evade capture.

Indestructible Bob made a very good recovery from the injuries he sustained at the hands of the nasty men, all of whom received hefty prison sentences apart from the nasty man who ran away, (the one who was pulled out of the wreckage of his car by Indestructible Bob.)

The man who had been pulled from the wreckage of his car by Indestructible Bob, phoned Indestructible Bob one evening.

"We'll get you eventually," he said. "There are many of us and you are but one. You are not indestructible you know."

"Yes, I am," said Indestructible Bob.

The nasty man who had been pulled out the wreckage of his car by Indestructible Bob was beginning to feel a little hysterical.

"No one is indestructible! If we won't get you, someone will! If nobody gets you, illness and old age will! You will die one day."

"My body will die eventually," agreed Indestructible Bob. "Flesh will wither and decompose. My brain will rot. But *I* won't die. My body is not who I am."

"Who *are* you then?" cried the nasty man who had been pulled out of the wreckage of his car some months previously.

"I am Indestructible Bob," said Indestructible Bob.

Laughing Gravy

Triratna InHouse Publications
www.*triratna-inhouse-publications.org*

TRIRATNA
INHOUSE
PUBLICATIONS

Printed in Great Britain
by Amazon